ARCANE OPS

ARCANE OPS

FEDERAL AGENTS OF MAGIC™ BOOK SEVEN

TR CAMERON   MARTHA CARR   MICHAEL ANDERLE

DISRUPTIVE IMAGINATION®

Copyright © 2019 TR Cameron, Martha Carr and Michael Anderle
Cover Art by Jake @ J Caleb Design
http://jcalebdesign.com / jcalebdesign@gmail.com
Cover copyright © LMBPN Publishing
A Michael Anderle Production

LMBPN Publishing
PMB 196, 2540 South Maryland Pkwy
Las Vegas, NV 89109

First US edition, August 2019
Version 1.01, December 2019
eBook ISBN: 978-1-64202-428-9
Print ISBN: 978-1-64202-429-6

ARCANE OPS - TEAM

Thanks to the JIT Readers

Jeff Goode
Daniel Weigert
Misty Roa
Dave Hicks
Diane L. Smith
Shari Regan
Larry Omans

If we've missed anyone, please let us know!

Editor
The Skyhunter Editing Team

DEDICATIONS

For Dylan

— *TR Cameron*

To everyone who still believes in magic
and all the possibilities that holds.
To all the readers who make this
entire ride so much fun.
And to my son, Louie and so many wonderful friends who
remind me all the time of what
really matters and how wonderful
life can be in any given moment.

— *Martha*

To Family, Friends and
Those Who Love
To Read.
May We All Enjoy Grace
To Live The Life We Are
Called.

— *Michael*

CHAPTER ONE

Ice shards hurtled at Diana from all directions, her attacker's abilities sufficiently impressive to threaten her from every angle. She responded with a raised-arm spin that created a shell of frozen power around her and drew energy from the matching magic when the icicles struck and failed to penetrate. She smiled through the barrier at the distorted view of her teacher, whose head looked to be about twice its normal size thanks to the fun-house-mirror effect of the ice. *Don't laugh. Seriously. Don't laugh.* Her internal self materialized in a corner of her mind and nodded agreement, equally aware that to laugh at the Dark Elf was to court one's own destruction.

But as her adversary moved and her head appeared to increase in size even more, the mirth escaped her control. The scowl it generated was three times worse than normal, as was the flaming wave she hurled at her student. Diana conjured her own fire sphere to intercept it but couldn't find a way out of the relentless assault to counter it. *Apparently, the lesson for today is how to maintain a defensive bubble.*

At least it's less tiring than usual. In the next moment, the attack vanished and she banished her defense, ready for the next.

When the tentacles erupted all around her opponent, she panicked for an instant. Her dislike of shadow was manageable but the tentacle version of the magic reached into her soul and suffused her with dread. She'd spent too much time dealing with the things—or trapped by them—to respond with the kind of rational detachment she needed to combat them.

Force blades materialized in her hands, and she slashed at the approaching appendages, not quite wildly but definitely not as calmly and deliberately as she might have preferred. Her teacher fired shadow orbs at her, and she swung the magical swords faster to intercept them while she fended off the grasping limbs. She managed to hold her own effectively, which gave her a second of pride that lasted only until the moment when Nylotte snuck a shadowy orb in at her feet and she missed the block.

The impact knocked her legs out from under her, and she managed to flop to her side as she fell with a solid thump. She staggered upright, ready to defend herself, but the Drow stood with her arms folded and stared at her.

The agent frowned. "What?"

Nylotte's voice was entirely matter of fact. "You need to be better."

"I'm well aware that I don't live up to your expectations, oh most honored master of the magical arts."

The other woman snorted. She looked extra prissy today, clad in a tight red dress that buttoned up the left side from the top of her knee-high black boots to her neck.

Her snowy hair was slicked back, and her dark skin shone in the flickering light of the basement. As always, Diana was underdressed in tactical pants, boots, and a concert t-shirt. Adam Ant's face stared from today's selection. Her own hair had been chopped to an inch to match the chunk that had been burned away in battle. When her teacher spoke again, it was still without judgment. "Your enemies grow stronger and increase in number. If you don't reach your full potential, they may defeat you."

"I'm sure you'd cry for days."

The Dark Elf raised an elegant eyebrow. "I have invested a great deal of time and energy on your behalf and opened myself to possible risk as well. Do not forget, your enemies attacked me directly."

Diana shook her head. "I believe they were your enemies, too. Correct me if I'm wrong, but Dreven seemed rather interested in you."

The other woman laughed. "Indeed so. Arranged marriages are such a bother. He was deeply offended when I chose not to agree to the practice."

Her jaw dropped but she gathered herself and decided there were some things she really didn't need to know. "So, how do I improve? It feels like I've come about as far as I can with fire, ice, lightning, and force. My telekinesis is fine. That leaves shadow, and we are both well aware that I'm hopeless at that."

"True." The Drow nodded. "More practice will enhance your existing skills, of course, but you are correct that the largest gains have already been accomplished. There are only two more paths for growth, and really, they are the same. A Rhazdon artifact, or Fury."

3

The idea of having one of the slimy, invasive artifacts—she was sure they would be slimy and simply knew it in her bones—working its way under her skin was a concept that made her nauseous whenever it occurred to her. She swallowed hard and replied, "The sword, then."

"The sword. Yes." Nylotte shrugged. "Well, we are done here for today. I will let you know when I have a new idea on where to pursue the final piece of Rhazdon's Vengeance."

She stepped into the portal her teacher created to send her home and noticed as she crossed over that the Drow wore a fierce scowl. *Damn. I hope that's not my fault.*

When the gentle but insistent request for connection had pressed against her mind, Nylotte had been both shocked and suspicious. She lowered her defenses only enough to receive the message, which allowed her to know the source and the content but permitted no further invasion. It was a sophisticated use of mental magic on her part, but decades of practice had made her an expert at protecting her consciousness from others. Her first thought in response involved a great deal of colorful language, and her second had been to get rid of her student as quickly as possible.

What on Earth and Oriceran would Iressa want to discuss with me? She and the other witch had never gotten along and even less so once the woman had entered the radius of Dreven's influence. The Drow had assumed, after the battle in the kemana, that all the supposedly secret members of the Remembrance circle had declared themselves her enemies. To have one seek her out so soon after that event was not an expected occurrence, to say the least.

She spoke the commands and made the required gestures to lock her shop and activate the defenses set throughout. After the building's unfortunate service as a battleground, she had updated everything and had brought craftspeople in to repair what had been broken. There were now more surprises awaiting an invader than there had been before, and she had ensured that the outer wards were as strong as she could make them.

She summoned a cushion and sat in the lotus position within her ward rings, inside the outermost but outside the innermost to limit the area where the other woman's magic would function. There was little doubt that Iressa would make similar arrangements or already had. She closed her eyes and stilled her mind before she locked onto the trace of energy the witch had left behind. She wove her own power into it and released it along the path to the other woman. The witch's image appeared in the center of the wards, also seated on a pillow She was dressed entirely in clinging black, as was her wont, and wore her typical smug expression.

Nylotte inclined her head and the witch spoke. "Thank you for accepting my request to speak."

"Of course. We are sisters, are we not?" Witches, long forced to defend themselves against the attempts of wizards to subordinate them, respected the connection their magic and the unified purpose of protecting their own power from others who would take it gave them. That history wouldn't be enough to keep her from killing the other woman, if necessary, but she'd think about it for a moment first. *Doubtless, she feels the same.*

The thin smile Iressa bestowed upon her confirmed it. Her pale skin was a stark contrast to her dress, but she had a little color in the cheeks as if she was energized by something. *And if it's good for her, it is likely not good for me, or Diana, or both.* Her voice was smooth and seductive, as always. "Nylotte, I wished to give you an opportunity to distance yourself from all this." She waved a negligent hand. "It is not your fight and there is no need for you to be involved in it."

"Dreven seemed to disagree."

A true smile broke out across the witch's features. "He did. But now, he is dead and those of us who knew him celebrate his end."

"Are you sure? He's cheated the reaper before."

Iressa showed her teeth in an even wider grin. "I was there. I saw the knife pierce his heart and can assure you he is gone. He probably deserved a more torturous farewell, but one cannot have it all, I suppose."

Nylotte nodded. "Very good. However, it is not up to you to determine what is, or is not, my fight."

The positive expression vanished as if it had never been, instantly replaced by a scowl. "What do you have to gain? The appreciation of the humans you surround yourself with? Have you truly forgotten yourself so much?"

Her reply was cold but level. "I'm not sure you're one to speak ill of my compatriots, Iressa. Your 'circle' was laughable, and your connection to the witch in the city above is beneath you. She is damaged goods, at the least, and more likely broken and insane."

The woman shrugged and her hair fell perfectly with the motion. *Iressa is always perfect.* "Regardless. You are at a moment of choice, Drow. You can choose to disengage from those I name my enemies and live your life free of my involvement. Or you can count yourself among them and face the consequences of that decision. Truly, I cannot imagine why you would consider doing the latter."

The Dark Elf smiled. "And yet, that is my choice. If it is between you and the people I have met here, there is no comparison. You are, at best, a clinging sycophant who mistakes the desire of powerful men to get into your pants for their respect for your power. You deserve the fate you have courted."

Iressa shook her head and a sad smile curved her lips. "Having been born unattractive, it's logical that you might not understand this, but what I have is both—their desire and their respect. The more powerful the witch or wizard, the more attracted they are to what I offer, and the more I can use them to further my ends. But plainly, you come up short on both measures—power and desirability. It must be so very difficult being you. Perhaps that is why you live underground as an outcast."

Nylotte grinned. "I look forward to watching you fall, Iressa—you and whatever master you serve now that Dreven is no more."

Her laughter was seductive, even with the Drow's very real dislike to temper it. "I never served Dreven, regardless of what I might have led him to believe. There were always plans behind plans, and more hidden behind those. He served his purpose and now, we will destroy you and your friends in flaming ruin. The game, until now, was simply to test and discern the edges of the battlefield." The witch shook her head. "From here on, I'm afraid, you will experience the result of your choices. And I do not expect you will like them."

She rolled her eyes. "Since they've required me to talk to you, I already dislike them. Vehemently." She canceled the connection and the woman's image evaporated before she could respond. The Dark Elf sighed, rose smoothly to her feet, and sent the cushion toward its resting place with a minor expenditure of magic. *I will need to warn Diana that we've poked the enemy sufficiently to anger them.* She snorted. *We're two of a kind, it seems, when it comes to our ability to irritate others.*

CHAPTER TWO

Cara shifted down a gear as she whipped around the curve. The motorcycle leaned beneath her as the engine wailed. Thanks to the newly installed version of Quinn in her helmet, she could have taken the roads faster if she'd chosen to rely on a little computer coaching. *But riding isn't about optimization, it's about exhilaration.* A corner of her display showed a view of the area surrounding her from above—about a fifth of a mile in each direction, courtesy of one of Kayleigh's drones. The tech had given Quinn the authority to access the watchers at will and the agent certainly didn't mind the potential warning of oncoming trouble.

Like the idiots in the train yard. She shook her head. *May all our enemies prove to be so incompetent.*

Unfortunately, the likelihood of that wish coming true was about equal to the possibility that if she leapt off the motorcycle, she would suddenly be able to fly. Dispatching Marcus had been necessary and even distantly rewarding, but she didn't fool herself that it was the end of the

Remembrance threat. If anything, it would likely become more pronounced now that they had been wounded. The bike bucked and she corrected the skid and downshifted again to bring the vehicle under control.

Her ride shuddered once more and without warning, she hurtled over the handlebars toward the pavement. She tucked her limbs and rolled as she impacted and skidded along the road. The loud crash from behind was easily attributed to her ride meeting the guardrail at high speed. She transitioned from hard surface to dirt as she slowed and crossed the threshold of the tree line at the edge of the small clearing with only a little momentum remaining.

Quinn's voice was urgent in her ears. "Don't move, puddin'. Scan underway."

She choked on the blood in her mouth and spat it to the side. "I'm not sure I could move if I wanted to." Parts of the left side of her body felt broken and she scrabbled for the healing potion at her hip. The cross-draw with her functioning arm proved to be a challenge but doable. She raised it to her lips as the AI informed her of the damage, some of which was quite severe, and braced for the rush of repair and the pain that would accompany it. Her mind lost its hold on consciousness during the process but when it was over, Quinn yelled at her until she regained her senses. The climb to her feet was shaky and involved a stagger or two but eventually, she was able to look around her with some semblance of clear thought. Her Arch KRGT-1 was a twisted mess and the waiting list to replace it was daunting. She snorted. *John Wick better get busy with his side gig.*

The red dot representing Hank—who had been the one to respond to Quinn's call for help—had grown notably closer while she took care of her injuries, and she waited impatiently for her ride home to arrive. It was a surprise when it took the form of a large black truck that rolled onto the shoulder beside the clearing. He swung down from the cab and walked over to regard her with his arms folded, looking appealingly muscular and vastly relieved. There had been a moment when she thought something might happen between them, but she'd quickly learned they weren't a good fit. Fortunately, she and Anik were and they'd spent quality time together on the sly.

She tugged her helmet off and set it aside before she frowned at the dirt that covered her heavy riding boots and jeans. Her leather jacket had taken the worst damage, with scrapes and tears now its most notable feature. She unzipped it and pulled it off to reveal her black ARES tunic, which had quickly become her favorite base layer. "Hey, Hercules, were you in the neighborhood?"

He shook his head with a laugh. "I was on the way back from getting this baby finished." One arm made an expansive gesture at the truck behind him. "It's ready."

Her eyes widened and she couldn't contain the grin. "Damn. That was fast."

Hank shrugged. "Many of the fight club guys are mechanics, as it turns out. They helped in exchange for a continuous flow of beer and bourbon."

Cara laughed. "So, everything is installed but it's all upside down, is that it?"

His laugh was filled with pride. "Everything is perfect, exactly as it should be. You know me. It couldn't be any other way." She did know him and he was undoubtedly correct. There was nothing in his records or in their history together that would suggest anything but the most complete diligence and competence from the big man. He tilted his chin at her former ride. "That's quite a mess you made."

She nodded. "Yeah. Something went wrong—other than the rider, I mean. There was a small lurch, followed by a big lurch, and I was suddenly a poorly aimed projectile." She stepped forward to clap him on the arm. "But we'll deal with that later. Show me the truck and show me now. Oh, the boss hasn't seen it yet, right?"

He shook his head. "Nope. I wanted you to be the first. I've only now picked it up from the final install of the skin. We had to go out of house for that. It's damn sophisticated stuff." He walked to the back of the vehicle and put his palm against a flat panel on one of the doors. They parted with a mechanical whir to reveal BAM Pittsburgh's long-awaited mobile armory.

Tiny lights flickered to life across the ceiling to provide a diffuse glow in the interior. It was grey on black and a bench ran down one side with lockers on the wall opposite. More storage space was present above the seat, high enough that even the tallest members of the team would be able to avoid concussion. In the portion nearest the cab, a stretcher and equipment were positioned ready for emergency medical support.

She whistled. "Damn, it's exactly what you said it would be. I thought it might have to lose some of the planned features once you really got into it."

Hank shook his head and looked proud. "I had to make some concessions, so while everything is large enough to suit its purpose, there's minimal room left over, but it all fit. Let me show you around." He pulled a folding step out of the bumper and climbed up. Cara followed, still amazed by the actual reality of the mobile armory she'd argued for —Diana would say whined about—since they'd started working in Pittsburgh.

Weapons racks were affixed to both sides as she entered. On the right were vertically stored rifles and shot-guns, one row above the other. On the left, a series of pistols stored grip-out was positioned between selections of grenades above and below. She selected a handgun and confirmed it was the agents' standard Glock-19. "Spare mags are in the lockers," he explained and led her deeper into the vehicle. He opened one and gestured at the gear inside. A complete outfit rested on a combination of hangers and shelves, including vest and AR glasses. "This is only a mockup. Once we decide who gets what locker, Kayleigh and I will put in a full set of custom kit."

Cara shook her head. "Damn, man. You have far, far exceeded my vision for this thing."

He grinned. "You haven't seen the half of it." He turned to the storage above the bench—which was only about a foot high—and slid the front panel up and over to reveal heavier weapons.

She frowned. "A missile launcher? Really?"

"You never know. It's better to have it and not need it than need it and be without."

Other pieces were in the overhead compartments as they moved toward the cab, including a disassembled mortar with a number of different shells. They appeared to be custom-built. She mentioned it, and he laughed.

"Kayleigh's added a few toys. I don't know what they all are, but I'm sure the boss does."

They passed through some kind of static field as they entered the medical area, and she shook her head. "Sterile?"

Hank looked offended and assumed a posh accent. "What an impertinent question. I am quite fertile, thank you." They laughed together, and he continued in his normal voice. "Not perfectly so but enough to at least knock off the big dirt. Our gear is protected against it."

"There isn't much room to work in. We'll have to hire a small medic."

His pride in the vehicle showed in his wide grin. "Not necessarily." He glanced upward. "Okay, Marvin, you can come out of hiding now."

A voice emanated from hidden speakers throughout the truck to add barely a hint of echo. It sounded like Alan Rickman from *Dogma*, uppity accent and all. "Welcome, Agent Binot."

"Uh…hi, Marvin." She looked at Hank. "Why Marvin?"

He shook his head despairingly. "Have you not seen *Hitchhiker's Guide to the Galaxy*? For shame."

"I prefer my Marvins to be Martian, thanks."

"Cretin."

"Jerk."

Marvin added, "If you are done being clever, allow me to take care of the…um, 'big reveal,' as Agent Stills calls it." Panels slid aside with a soft hiss, and a robot arm unfolded from the ceiling over the stretcher, while another extended from the front wall of the truck. They spun and rotated to display the wide array of equipment built into the ends of each—scalpels, needles, and a host of other scary-looking implements. "I am a fully functional trauma medic."

She realized her jaw was hanging open and pulled it shut, then turned to stare at Hank. "How?"

He grinned. "I still have some military contacts. This took a big push from the higher-ups, though. I only got our foot in the door. It's in testing, so we get to be part of that."

"I'll stick with healing potions."

"Oh, I think we all will. But there's always the possibility that we'll run out or that someone might, say, crash their motorcycle due to bad piloting and need treatment."

Marvin interrupted her snarky reply. "I have communicated with Quinn, Agent Binot's AI. The issue in this particular incident was not skill-related. The vehicle was struck by two bullets—the first in the exhaust pipe, and the second in the front wheel. It would have been impossible to avoid a crash."

They exchanged alarmed glances before Cara asked, "Do we know who did it?"

"The aerial coverage did not reveal anyone, and the shooter was beyond the range of the cameras mounted on your helmet and motorcycle." She thought she detected a note of frustration in his voice. *I have to be making that up, though. The AIs aren't that good. Well, other than Quinn.*

"Dammit."

Hank affirmed her opinion. "And double damn it, too. Marvin, put the word out to everyone to be on the lookout. Mention to the boss that she might consider kicking the warning up the ladder, too."

"Done."

Cara sighed and swung out of the truck to retrieve her

helmet, gave the wreckage of her bike one last forlorn look, and sighed again. As she turned to Hank, he leapt cleanly from the vehicle, collapsed the stairs into their storage position, and palmed the sensor to close the doors. He swiveled to face her and offered a broad smile. "So, lady, do you need a lift?"

"I guess I do. It's quite a ride you have here."

He tilted his chin up. "And I didn't even mention the stuff on the roof."

"What stuff on the roof?"

He laughed considerably during the drive back to the base so she could pick up one of the ARES vehicles but didn't reveal anything else about the truck despite her cleverest attempts to coax it out of him. *Oh, well. I guess I'll find out when I need to.*

CHAPTER THREE

R ath twisted and hurled two knives he held in his right hand. The blades flew unerringly across the garage to embed themselves in the new targets Chan had hung since their previous practice session there. They were the last blades he carried in the sheaths strapped to his ribs, although he still had the one at his lower back his teacher had given him when they'd first begun working together. His new ones were as high-tech and perfect as Kayleigh and Emerson could make them, so he wore the original as a talisman that connected him to his training rather than a weapon to use.

The older man clapped. "Well done, Rath. Six for six. It is clearly time we found something more challenging for you."

The troll grinned at the praise and the joy of working with the weapons master. "Throw all six at once?"

A laugh accompanied the reply. "No, not that. You already have those skills, based on what you've accomplished so far. I have no doubt you could hit whatever you threw at. But what if you couldn't see your foe?"

Rath frowned when he realized such a situation was highly relevant to his hearing-impaired teacher. There were movies he'd seen, of course, where the hero was taught to battle blindfolded. He chuckled inwardly and imagined himself whining like a certain future Jedi. *I can't even see. How am I supposed to fight?* Somehow, he didn't think Chan would appreciate the complaint.

He caught the cloth his mentor threw and tied it around his head. The man retrieved his knives and slid them into their sheaths with small pushes. Rath ran his fingers along them in a newly developed habit to confirm that all six were in place and ready for easy access. He let his arms hang at his sides while he waited. The sounds of the room became more prominent and the hum of the air conditioning almost overwhelmed the sound of the traffic that passed outside. He started when Chan spoke from much closer than he'd expected.

"I will make my way through the garage. When you think you can hit me, throw. Don't worry about hurting me. I'll be fine."

The student frowned, not sure whether that was a commentary on his skills or on his teacher's, but let any concern slide away. *If I'm not good at this now, I will be soon. That's what counts.* He crouched slightly, turned toward where he'd last heard the man, and shifted his feet as quietly as he could so he would hear any clue that might present itself. *Dagnabit. I don't remember where stuff is in the room. Stupid. Another mistake never to make again.* He heard a sound from ahead and to his left, and he drew and hurled a blade backhand. It clattered as it struck something that definitely wasn't his target.

Chan's instruction was calm, serious, and nonjudgmental. "That was a good attempt. You were within a couple of feet of me. If you'd been in balance when you threw, you might have hit true. Don't overreact. Stay focused."

Rath was tempted to cheat and throw while the man talked, but only for an instant. He rotated in that direction and listened carefully. The scuff of a shoe on the concrete floor caught his attention, and he made a mental note of its location but held back from attacking. When the next sound came, he was able to determine the possible line of travel and drew two blades. He threw one where his target would be if he'd stopped and the other to where he'd be if he kept moving. His teacher clapped loudly. "Excellent work. If I had not been crouched, you would have had me."

Drat. Right. Aim lower. Another sound alerted him and he deliberately reacted to that one, hurled a blade with his left hand, and listened carefully for movement in response. He heard a faint footfall under the sound when the first knife clattered into the wall and threw with his right. Another clap greeted his effort and his teacher's voice was pleased. "Remove the blindfold." He complied and saw the man standing with his palms pressed together in front of him, the blade trapped between them and only inches from his chest. "That was a perfect throw."

He grinned. "Fun. More?"

Chan returned the grin. "Oh, definitely. That was mostly luck. We need to practice until luck is irrelevant."

"Teach me to catch knives?"

His teacher laughed. "You have to walk before you can run, my friend. We'll get there."

The troll squinted as he left the garage. When he'd arrived, it had been bright daylight. Now, dusk was falling and coated his teacher's neighborhood in shadows and grey haze. It was a fairly long walk home. While he usually enjoyed the journey, there was something about tonight's ominous sky that made him uneasy. He checked to make sure his batons were ready in his backpack and that he could reach his knives under the light coat he wore to conceal them. In the early days of his training, the blades rode in the pack as well. The Remembrance attack on Cara at the train yard had inspired them all to pay more attention to security, however, and he now kept what weapons he could at hand.

Gwen played DJ for him, spinning songs he didn't yet know but that she thought he'd like into his earphones. She was right at least two-thirds of the time and sometimes hit a streak. She was in the middle of one now with something she called "surf rock" that had great drums in it. He bounced along to the happy rhythms, greeted people he passed, and generally enjoyed himself as he crossed into the outer part of the neighborhood that surrounded the house he shared with Diana and Kayleigh.

An unexpected voice interrupted the music. "Troll, don't you think it's time you paid your respects to those who have gone before?"

It was scratchy, heavily modulated, and unidentifiable. Paradoxically, those simple facts made it abundantly clear who it was. *Amadeo. How did he get into my comms? Kayleigh will be upset.*

"What?" The man didn't reply, and Rath realized he'd stopped walking without intending to. He glanced to his right, saw the graveyard he always passed on this route, and decided that was what the man must be referring to. *Drat. Being predictable in my route home.* He'd not visited the cemetery before and in the darkness, its layout looked confusing.

With his comms compromised, he couldn't call for backup or even ask Gwen for a map without the assassin knowing. He dithered for only a moment before he turned and entered. The man hadn't shown any inclination to hurt him at their previous meetings and there was no reason to think that had changed. If it had, he could have let him know he was present with a bullet, rather than a message. A path stretched ahead, sufficiently wide for two people to walk beside one another, and headstones filled the grassy areas on either side. A light winked, caught in his peripheral vision, and he swung in that direction. When he moved close enough to make it out, he discovered the object of his search seated on the steps of the largest building in sight, which appeared to be a family mausoleum of some kind.

When he came within earshot, Amadeo spoke, his voice still distorted to preserve his anonymity. "Times are becoming dangerous for you and yours, troll." Even without the normal tones to judge by, it sounded like an observation, not a threat.

Rath fingered the knives on his left ribs with his right hand but still sensed no imminent danger. When he got closer, he discovered that the assassin was dressed for trouble in an outfit that mostly resembled the ARES combat kit plus a mask that covered his face. *Or maybe that's how he spends all his time. Who knows?* "What danger?"

The synthesized laugh was eerie. "It seems like all kinds of danger. Crazy half-robots, insane witches, evil men from another planet, and now, simply for fun, bounty hunters and assassins."

"Like you?"

"Never. I limit myself to eliminating criminals who deserve their end. None of you fit that description. Yet, at least."

The troll halted his approach when he reached the bottom of the stairs and folded his arms. "Who, then?"

Amadeo spread his hands wide. "Anyone who's anyone among this town's criminal element, really. The news is out. There are bounties offered for the two leaders of your group, dead or alive."

"By who?"

He shrugged. "An unnamed party. This is normally handled by word of mouth and the underworld grapevine, so it's unlikely that you'll be able to track the source. But it's not that hard to guess, is it?"

Rath shook his head. "Many possibles." With a frown, he asked, "Anyone other than those two?"

"Not on the bounty list. But you can probably assume that everyone connected to them is in danger of one kind or another."

Double drat. He knew he had to ask the next question

but really didn't want to. In the silence before he could bring himself to speak, the assassin stood suddenly and he had to force himself to remain still. "Why do you care?" he blurted.

The tall man looked at him, any revelations his expression might provide hidden behind the featureless black mask he wore and behind the flat black plastic triangles that obscured his eyes. His body language communicated nothing other than a permanent readiness as if he were always seeking an edge against anyone who might consider confronting him.

When he spoke, his voice was deep and harsh, the masking device apparently deactivated. He sounded older than Rath would have expected. "I know I am a bad man who does bad things. It's a choice I've made, and I am content with it and whatever results from it. But that doesn't mean I can stand by and let harm find those who do not deserve to come to harm. You and your people are good, and I am obligated to assist."

"By who?"

He laughed, and the machine hiding his voice activated to remove the mirth from the sound and left only a harsh buzz. "By the only person fit to judge my actions, troll. By me." He strode around the edge of the building and out of sight, and by the time Rath dashed over, he had vanished into the darkness.

"Gwen, warn Cara and Diana of new danger."

"Done."

"Have drone deliver gear. We need to check on Griffins and go patrol."

"Affirmative. Ten minutes."

The troll nodded and crouched to wait. *The graveyard would make a good superhero lair. Wonder if there are any zombies around for target practice.*

CHAPTER FOUR

Even though Iressa had expected a summons from Dreven's patron, it was still a surprise when it arrived. That the person was aware of where she lived was troubling, and the fact that he had chosen such a beautiful piece of jewelry to include with the invitation revealed how much he knew about her. There was ample time between the delivery and the moment indicated in the elegant note that had accompanied the gift for her to prepare. Her first act was to investigate the fancy broach with every magical tool at her disposal. She finally confirmed it as an inert token rather than something that would come to life and attack her at his command.

Most likely, anyway. One couldn't be entirely sure about such things. But leaving it behind wasn't an option as it would offer him an excuse to take offense, which might give him an excuse to engage in far more unpleasant undertakings in response. She visited her walk-in closet and selected a long black dress that covered her to her calves and knee-high boots. It required a significant amount of wriggling to get the outfit properly into place, but there was no way she would go into this meeting without her best battledress. She sat before her mirror and checked her hair, which flowed perfectly over her shoulders, and applied a little color to her lips and cheeks.

The witch selected the rarest bottle from her array of perfumes, sprayed some on her neck and wrists, and inhaled, appreciating the spicy notes of the scent. She slipped on a thigh holster, swiveled it to the back so she could still walk in the tight sheath, and put her backup wand into it. Her main one slid neatly into the jeweled holder sewn into the arm of the dress. He'd know about that one, so there was no reason to hide it.

A shiny black leather belt that rode low on her hips finished the look. A touch in the familiar locations confirmed the presence of hidden potions and other toys masquerading as ornaments. He might see through that, too, but there was no way she would walk onto his battlefield without them. *If he doesn't like it, he can always rescind my invitation. But I think he probably needs me more than I need him, at this point.* Finally, she pinned the broach to her dress at her left shoulder, where its representation of a jeweled dragon in green, gold, and red set off the ensemble perfectly. With a nod and an exhalation, Iressa rose to start the evening's entertainment.

She summoned the portal and stepped through to a location outside a locked gate in front of a large plot of land. A castle stood in the distance, doubtless his home and her ultimate destination. In the falling darkness, it loomed like a living thing with a multitude of winking eyes showing through the curtains. She rejected the notion of playing this particular game and cast a spell that would allow her to see the structure's entrance clearly. The witch opened her senses to catalog the barriers that would seek to prevent her from going directly toward it and smiled when she discovered they weren't sophisticated enough to deter her. Another portal, carefully woven to avoid his outer defenses, deposited her on the porch at the closed double doors.

They swung open silently before her and a shimmer along the deep-red carpet that lay in the center of the corridor indicated her path forward. She progressed slowly and took time to inspect the sparsely placed but beautiful and rare items of art that decorated the spacious hall. The tapestries on the walls, by contrast, were bloody remembrances of battles long past, and her lip curled in distaste at the mundanity.

A number of twists and turns finally brought her to a lavish den with a roaring fireplace and two large wingback chairs facing it on either side of a low table. A crystal decanter containing a dusky liquid and two elegant glasses stood on its surface, and a pale hand rested on the inside arm of the left chair. She circled to the right and his greeting was filled with amusement under the heavy rasp of his tone.

"Iressa, welcome. What a shame you chose not to wander through the field and appreciate the marvel of the building. Dreven never missed the opportunity to do so."

She completed her approach and paused, momentarily

speechless at the sight of him. He appeared to be undistinguished in build, aside from looking slightly underfed. The scars that crossed his face, emphasized with scarlet tattoos, caught the eye and refused to release it. He radiated power, even in his casual position, and his red-tinted eyes burned as if they could barely restrain it. His simple trousers and shoes surprised her, but a red-and-gold jacket looked like it would feel luscious to the touch. Black hair swept back on the top and sides.

Iressa lowered herself into the chair with a smile that displayed confidence she no longer felt. The aura of menace that emanated from the master of the castle battered at her mind and set her ill at ease. "I guess I'm less interested in games than dear departed Dreven was."

He raised a black eyebrow and his scars stretched and twisted with the movement. "I was, of course, aware that Dreven had left this plane of existence. I didn't know word had spread, however."

Shit. Either I'm imagining that suspicious tone or he's convinced I was involved. To say the least. As always, the memory of Dreven's last moments brought a smile. She raised her brow in an echo of his gesture. "He hasn't annoyed me in over a week. That alone tells me he must be dead. He could never avoid being an irritant for that long, otherwise."

His dark laughter conveyed his disbelief in her explanation and his lack of concern over it. "Speaking ill of the deceased is uncouth."

"Not if the deceased is—was—uncouth."

A thin smile settled on his lips as he inclined his head. "Well said. However, I asked you to come here for reasons other than wordplay. The broach looks beautiful on you, by the way."

The abrupt change of direction left her momentarily off-balance. "Thank you, it was a very thoughtful gesture on your part."

He waved a hand. "To business, then. Dreven was my pawn in matters on Earth. With him off the board, I find myself in need of another champion."

"Certainly not another pawn, however."

Lechnas grinned. "Certainly not. Dreven was too deeply flawed to rise higher. You, however, could be a bishop, at least."

She scowled at the taunt. "Many have underestimated me. Each has paid a substantial price for doing so. You may want to consider whether you wish to be among them."

He gestured at the pin on her shoulder. "Surely I have already paid."

Iressa laughed. "Surely I cannot be bought for trinkets or for palaces. Only power suits."

Instead of responding, he poured the liquid from the decanter into both glasses and offered them to her. She chose the one on the left and waited until he drank from his own before sipping. It was bourbon—in the top five of her favorite tastes from Earth—and of the highest quality, at that. She nodded in appreciation, took another sip, and set it down before she focused on him.

He sighed and did the same. "Were we to enter into a partnership, I would hold the superior position, always. Is that an arrangement you would be comfortable with?"

"But of course." *Until I kill you.* "Your power exceeds mine." *At the moment.*

His smile suggested that he heard the unspoken words and was as unconcerned with them as he was with Dreven's fate. "In that case, then, allow me to be blunt. What do you have to offer me?"

A flurry of answers ranging from flirtatious to outraged flipped through her mind, each quickly discarded. She leaned forward and saw his gaze flick to the low-cut neck of her dress and suppressed a grin. *So, you're not as detached as you'd like to pretend. Good.* "With the proper support, I can accomplish any goals we may set ourselves. However, I require a significant degree of autonomy."

He nodded. "I wouldn't have it any other way. I have enough to occupy my attention on this planet."

"Dreven never revealed he was working for someone else. In fact, he didn't share any plan beyond simply gaining power on Earth. I assume you have additional plans that he either failed to share or wasn't aware of?"

He rose and gestured for her to do the same. "I do, and if we are truly to be partners, I will share them all with you."

She pushed herself to her feet and paused only to swallow the rest of her drink. "When do we start?"

He summoned a portal, and she peered into it to see that it led to the street outside her home. "As soon as you show me you can manage things on Earth. Step in for Dreven. Lead the magicals and the humans against the forces that oppose them and sow chaos. We have stood in one place too long. This city shall burn, as must every city that supports a kemana that refuses to submit."

Her eyes widened at the scope of his plan, and she smiled with true pleasure at the opportunities ahead. "I have one question. Why not simply eliminate Lady Alayne instead?"

He grinned and bared his teeth in the most intimidating look she'd seen from him. "Darling Iressa. Where would the fun be in that?"

CHAPTER FIVE

S arah had been at the warehouse when the insistent pressure in her mind told her Iressa wished to speak to her. She sighed contentedly, lifted her boots from where they rested on the office desk, and set them on the floor with a thump. Since Marcus and Dreven had both met their well-deserved ends, her life had improved a hundred-fold. The new human leader, Murray, was far more pliable and far less capable than his predecessor had been. And, better still, he clearly felt threatened by her magic and the abilities of her followers, which meant the balance of power in the Remembrance gang had finally shifted to its proper position.

She'd chosen not to reveal the existence of their new patron, content to let the others believe she was at the top of the chain. It increased their respect and their distance, both of which suited her. With a flick of her wand, she drew a rift in the air and stepped through it to the parking garage under her building. She had learned to manipulate the electronics of the elevator with magic and could turn every ride into a personal express trip if she willed it so, which meant she was in her apartment in under a minute.

The statuette that had connected her to Dreven rested on her glass coffee table, pierced with tiny holes she'd blasted into it for fun while she watched a movie. Each new wound on the item was like one more dagger stabbed into the man she still despised. She looked forward to reducing it to powder, piece by satisfying piece. But for now, such diversions would have to wait.

She kicked her boots off, lay down on the couch, and arranged herself comfortably. A twitch of her wand moved the table several feet away—a sensible precaution since sometimes, her new superior enjoyed ending their sessions in ways that caused her to thrash and fall when she reentered her body. That risk was why she had abandoned a respectful upright posture in favor of making sure she was horizontal before she reached out to Iressa. *It's petty but undeniably effective.* In the other witch's place, she'd have done the same. One final movement of her wand activated the wards that protected the condo from prying eyes and ears.

She composed her mind, let her eyes drift closed, and allowed the summons to wash over her. Her vision went truly dark, a fearful moment of transition that always seemed on the verge of stretching to eternity, before the world around her slid into place with a lurch that felt like she might stumble. Unlike their previous meetings, which had been in rather generic outdoor settings, a room enclosed her. Two black leather lounge couches were set at a right angle to one another, and her patron lay on her back on the farthest, sheathed as usual in her tight ebony dress. The walls and other features were blurred and indistinguishable. A hand gestured at the couch beside her, and Sarah crossed to take it, mimicking the other woman's position. Above her, the ceiling was fashioned of ornamental tiles in varying shades of white and off-white.

Iressa sounded relaxed and happy. "Thank you for coming so quickly."

"Of course. Now that I'm rid of the half-man, my freedom has notably increased."

The other woman laughed. "We are both rid of those who have vexed us for so long. It is a cause for celebration."

"Is that why you summoned me?"

"Hardly. Up until now, your group has not been a rousing success." She made a noise of protest, and Iressa shushed her. "No, no, I know it's not your fault. You have never had sufficient authority to achieve what is needed. You do not need to defend yourself to me. I only mention it because that time is behind us, which is another reason to celebrate."

Above her, a mist coalesced as if from nowhere and an image appeared. She frowned at the sight of the aerial view of Stonesreach. "I thought the kemana was all Dreven's doing?"

"We both thought that, and we were both incorrect. It turns out that his master wishes to claim all of them and to destroy those that will not surrender. As well as the cities above that harbor them, of course."

Sarah shook her head as the image burst into flames and the buildings burned to the ground as she watched. She was silent for a time, not sure how to respond. The witch was talking about destroying her home, the city she'd claimed as her own decades before. Finally, she shrugged. *Whatever. There are other cities. I hear Columbus, Ohio, is pleasant.* "Then destroy them both we shall. How would you like to proceed?"

The other witch's laughter was seductive, as always. "We will begin where you started long ago—by acquiring as many magical artifacts and items as we can. Surely some are housed nearby?"

"It is very likely. The ones the authorities have taken are probably in their police stations or in a warehouse awaiting the slow process of their legal system."

"Good. That is a place to start. We will gather power, gather people, and act when the moment is right."

Sarah asked, "Do I have complete authority over the group now, or will you make yourself visible?"

"You do. There is no need for them to be aware of me at this time—or, perhaps, at any time. Let the lines of power be clear to them."

"Excellent. I have felt for a while that the authorities somehow know too much about us. It was in my mind that Marcus was possibly a traitor and hindered the success of the group in order to bolster his own position. Hopefully, we will now discover whether that was the case or not."

The other woman's voice turned cold. "If you suspect anyone in the future, kill them. Humans are plentiful."

The witch's grin stretched her face. "Perfect."

For once, the transition back to her apartment was gentle, and she closed her eyes again and decided that the most appropriate form of celebration was a long nap.

Kayleigh straightened with a groan. From the moment Alfred had warned her that there was activity in the enemy leader's home, she'd listened in live from the devices Rath had seeded throughout the apartment. The visuals offered nothing, only the enemy witch lying on her couch, but it was clear when she spoke that a conversation took place, even though only one side of it was audible.

The mention of a police station or a warehouse had made her worried. But when Sarah followed it up with a concern about a traitor in their midst, Kayleigh had transitioned almost instantly to panic. She hurried through her lab area and entered Deacon's to tap him on the shoulder and draw his attention from the data on his screens and the music in his earphones. He pulled them down and tilted his head back to look up at her.

"Hey, blondie, what's happening?"

She gave him a gentle slap on the side of his skull and plopped into the chair beside him. "Do you have a way into police evidence inventories?"

He nodded. "Sure. It was a simple sidestep into them once we were given access to everything else."

"So they know you're in there?"

Deacon scratched the back of his neck and affected a neutral expression. "Well, I maybe wouldn't go quite that far."

"So much the better. Can you see where any magical items or artifacts that were taken from the Remembrance idiots are being held?"

He leaned forward and went to work, tapping his keyboard and touch interface. Although he muttered as he worked, she couldn't distinguish any chains of words that made sense. After a few minutes, he relaxed and pointed to his monitor, where a map of the city was displayed with several small red boxes scattered around it and one large rectangle off to one side. "There are a few low-power items everywhere—those are the smaller markers—but anything near or at artifact level taken from the Remembrance is held in a main location, the station closest to the courthouse."

Kayleigh sighed. "Way to make it easy for them."

"Well, that makes it easier for us, too, right?" he countered. "If they were spread all over the city, we'd have more places to defend."

"I don't want to have to defend anything. These people need to be shut down hard. I'm not sure why we shouldn't simply dive in and arrest them all when they're at the warehouse."

Her colleague shook his head. "You do know why but you simply can't admit that you're impatient. They've proven over and over that there are cells working in the city that they can activate at need. If we hit them hard, there's no telling what those other folks will do. The boss is right on this subject—we need to keep them on the line until they over-extend and we can destroy them all. Maybe this will be the opportunity that gets it done."

"No way. They won't commit everyone to breaking and entering to steal stuff."

"Well, you know, that kind of reinforces my point."

"Well, you know, you suck."

He laughed. "Way to finish off your argument. You're definitely rocking the logic, sister."

She stood and lashed out with a kick that made him

yelp when it connected with his shin. "I'm going to see what security they have around that place. Why don't you start working up a defense plan we can present to the field agents?"

"Your wish is my command, oh great one."

"Bite me."

The teasing worked, though, and she returned to her lab a little lighter in spirit than when she'd left it.

CHAPTER SIX

W hen Tony had shared a quiet word about the potential attack on the station with the police chief, her first reaction had been disbelief. She'd moved quickly from there to deep anger and given him the run of the place with orders to coordinate the defense based upon his prior PD experience and his current position with ARES. Kayleigh had monitored Sarah discussing the plan— seemingly to herself in her empty apartment—and knew it was planned for an unspecified time within the next eight hours.

The agents had considered and abandoned the notion of a preemptive strike against the Remembrance goons en route to the station. The witch's comment about the authorities knowing things they shouldn't had spooked them all. Kayleigh was adamant that they couldn't do anything to jeopardize Sloan's cover, and the rest of them had conceded with varying degrees of reluctance. The final outcome of their planning was that Tony, Anik, and Hank now pretended to be police to assist in the defense because

Cara and Diana were too recognizable. Even if there weren't bounties on them, their magic was a dead giveaway. The two techs ran drone overwatch but would be unable to provide much more than early warning without drawing additional suspicion.

One advantage was that they'd been able to bring Starsky and Hutch along. James Maxis and Vicki Greene had been on multiple bounty runs with the team and while unaware of the Security Agency's connection to ARES, were more than willing to participate in the defense of the station. They had also replaced most of the ordinary patrol officers with SWAT in disguise, and everyone nonessential had been sent home. They were as ready to defend the precinct as they could be. Now, it was merely a matter of waiting.

Tony completed his walkthrough of the second floor and secured the doors leading to the stairwells. They'd emptied and blocked off the top three floors, leaving only the entrance level and the basement accessible. The techs had a drone positioned high above, so if their foes did something unexpected and breached in one of the upper levels, they would know about it as soon as it happened. But what he didn't want was the Remembrance idiots running free through the building and thus securing the stairs. The lobby was filled with a few ordinary volunteer officers who would flee at the sight of an oncoming riot and throw the facility into lockdown as per standard procedures. When the enemy broke through, the fun would begin.

He joined his team in the center of the first floor. They were each responsible for a corner, with the two borrowed police officers working together on the fourth. They'd considered operating as a group but had again abandoned the preferred tactical choice in an effort to avoid giving the enemy any clues about Sloan. *That situation needs to be resolved fast. I hope the boss realizes that. I certainly don't want to be the one to bring it up.* He laughed quietly. *I'll mention it to Kayleigh and hide.*

As if thinking about her had been a catalyst, the tech spoke over the comms. "Incoming. They're not being subtle about it either. There are five vans and the heat signatures indicate twenty-three bodies including the drivers."

Anik shook his head. "More than we expected and less than we dreaded. They must have both magicals and street soldiers in there." One of their faint hopes had been that the enemy wouldn't include magical backup—which was ludicrous, of course, but that was how hope worked sometimes.

Tony replied, "The more they bring, the more we arrest and the fewer there are to deal with later." He keyed the button to add the non-ARES defenders into the conversation. "Incoming—approximately twenty-three, both magicals and not. The current plan stands." He nodded to his team and moved forward toward the entry area, which was his corner of responsibility. Anik broke right and Hank left. The other two faded to the rear.

The first sign that things wouldn't go as expected was when the raiders separated rather than enter the lobby as a group. The techs fed the image into their glasses, and they watched as separate teams took positions on each side of the building.

"Could we have spotted them somehow?" Hank asked. "Because zapping them with a drone would be a really easy way to end this."

Kayleigh snapped, "No," and Tony sighed. *Sloan has become a liability rather than a benefit. He has to come out from undercover.* He thrust the worry aside and focused on the situation. "We're not equipped for life on easy mode, Hercules. We'd be bored." The laughter—both from the ARES agents and the PD SWAT officers—ceased abruptly when the enemy launched a coordinated attack from all directions.

Huge explosions echoed as stone shattered inward at the midpoint of all four sides of the building. They ducked for cover, and Tony fed his camera over the desks he crouched behind. A team of five entered through the nearest wall, three with wands and two with rifles. They turned and moved toward his corner.

"Let them get inside, then engage when the moment seems right," he whispered. "We only have one moment of surprise." Technically, the officers waiting on the basement level would be a surprise as well, but that was merely semantics. He yanked the pins from two tear gas grenades —the only kind they could use with deniability—and lobbed them at the invaders. They landed but had no sooner begun to spray before they were hurled outside through the hole in the wall. "Dammit," he muttered under his breath, darted ahead in a crouch parallel to the enemy's advance, and hid behind cubicles as he tracked their progress.

They moved with unexpected discipline—significantly more than the other times when they'd engaged the gang.

Gunfire rang out from Anik's area of the floor, and Tony took it as a signal to dart up and fire a volley of bullets at the nearest targets. The rounds spun in midair and rocketed back toward him, and he crouched to avoid them.

"Okay, everyone, they've revealed themselves. Switch to anti-magic bullets." This was another decision made to hide their foreknowledge of the event. His magazine exchange was smooth and he raised the rifle again in time to see a wash of flame directed at his face. He ducked hastily and dashed along the aisle of desks, grimacing at the heat when the fire struck the desks behind him. The sprinklers activated to add an annoying new dimension to the battle. He continued his forward movement but headed in a zig-zag diagonal toward the front corner and its staircase, kept his head low, and trusted that the general noise around him would obscure his passage.

When the desks before him elevated and swung away to reveal a wizard who pointed a wand and a hoodlum with a rifle aimed squarely at him, Tony realized he'd been considerably less sneaky than he'd thought.

―――――――

When the enemy broke through the wall, Hank found an excellent place to hide and watched as those nearest to him formed a line and began to jog toward his assigned corner. A magical took the lead, followed by a rifle-holder, and a man with a shotgun trailed two more magicals. *Good choice. I should have brought a shotgun.* It really was a pointless thought because the model of shotgun he preferred would have revealed the defenders as more than ordinary police.

He circled quickly and quietly and fired at the line from the rear. The one at the back jerked and fell, his bulletproof vest useless against the bullets that caught him in the arms and legs as the agent swung the weapon up and down. The man's scream alerted the others and they scattered. The witch now at the rear used her magic to hurl a desk at him. Water from the sprinklers made the floor slick and he slipped when he dodged but still managed to evade the heavy projectile. It pounded into the wall behind him as he repositioned. Shouts receded toward the stairwell, and he cursed when he realized his quarry was getting away.

The agent took a deep breath, changed the magazine in his rifle, and darted out from cover. The invaders had split their forces and the witch who'd thrown the furniture and the rifleman waited for him. He sprayed a hasty barrage at them and received several strikes in the vest in return before a blast of force catapulted him against the wall. He tumbled as he fell and the magical energy surged through him. His talent was unique, as far as he knew, because it required him to give or take damage in order to invoke it, but it was always a thrill when it sparked to life. Hank surged forward with magically enhanced speed and planted the butt of his weapon in the face of the witch, who was clearly shocked that her magic hadn't stopped him. He aimed a kick at the knee of his second adversary as he brought the rifle around.

The joint cracked and the man fell with a wail and landed hard a second after the witch. He bound them together with zip ties, snapped the woman's wand in two, and threw the pieces away. The sounds of battle resounded from every area of the floor as the ARES agents and their allies battled the invaders. He considered, for only a moment, charging into the fray to assist the others. The loud slam of the stairwell door banished the thought from his mind, though, and he rushed forward after his quarry, only to discover that the barrier wouldn't budge. He gave it a kick, put all his magical energy into it, and only managed to dent the metal. *Damn. Good construction, police people.* "Khan, Stark, they've secured the stairwell going down somehow. I can't break through."

After a few moments' pause, Tony confirmed that the situation was the same on his side. Anik replied, "Clear these idiots who have me trapped and I'll get us through." Hank raced in that direction, and from the sounds of pistols fired in quick succession, Tony approached from another angle doing his gunslinger impersonation. They arrived together with Starsky and Hutch close behind them and quickly eliminated the witches and wizards that had kept the demolitions expert pinned down.

Anik rushed forward to the corner and Hank turned to the police officers. "Is everything okay on your end?"

Greene pulled her helmet off and ran a hand across her sweaty brow as she shook her head. "We tried to engage, but they kept us down and moved to the stairwell too fast. We got two but the rest made it through."

Maxis asked, "Why don't they simply portal in?"

Hank shrugged. "They have to know where they're going, is how I understand it. As in they need an anchor of some kind to connect to."

Greene laughed. "Otherwise, they wind up inside a rock or something, right? I'm sure I've seen that in a movie."

Maxis added, "Or *Star Trek*."

Anik announced, "Take cover," and dashed past them. They followed and hid behind an overturned desk as he detonated the explosives he'd placed.

Hank stood and grinned at a giant hole in the wall beside the door. "Nice."

The ARES demolition man shrugged. "They can ward or secure the door all they want, but people usually don't do the same for the walls. That one was heavy block but fortunately, not essential to the building's structural integrity."

Tony chuckled. "Okay, whatever. We can talk shop later. Get down the stairs. Starsky and Hutch, rear guard."

The large man led the way down the staircase with the former detective on his heels. They found the door to the basement level unsecured, which was unexpected. However, that wasn't nearly as surprising as the complete darkness and silence that greeted them when he opened it, rather than the expected sounds of battle.

"I have a bad feeling about this," Anik muttered. "Hercules, you go first."

His teammate, still in the lead, nodded. "Good plan. You all stay here until I say otherwise." He tapped the toggle on his glasses to activate low-light mode and took a step forward into the silent shadows.

CHAPTER SEVEN

Hank dialed his comms reception to the lowest perceptible setting and amplified the audio pickups to search for any sound in the basement. The hallway ahead was rendered in greens, blacks, and grays as the night-vision function, assisted by computing technology in the glasses, turned absolute darkness into twilight. He took several cautious steps forward before the first figure came into sight—a SWAT officer face-down on the floor. The woman's pulse was strong but when he rolled her over and shook her shoulder, he failed to rouse her.

"I found a SWAT," he whispered. "She's out cold but seems otherwise unharmed. I'll keep going. Stand by." The lower level's outer hallway tracked the perimeter of the building with entries toward the inner section at intervals. When the first swam into his vision, he placed his back against the wall and extended the camera from his left sleeve to poke it around the corner above head height. The room beyond was dark as well, but there was a glimmer in the door that led from it, he assumed deeper into the facility.

"Glam, map overview please." The view of the basement's layout appeared in a window on the far side of his display with a pulsing dot that indicated his position. *Okay, so the evidence room is still a couple of rooms in and to the right. That's where they'll probably be.* His adrenaline spiked as he connected the recent conversation with the present moment. *Shit. They don't have to fight their way out. They can merely portal everything away once they're in there unless there are anti-magic emitters nearby.*

He didn't waste any more precious seconds worrying about it but slipped into the room. His glasses adjusted as the light increased to provide an optimal view at all times. Two SWAT agents lay on the floor, slumped behind desks they apparently used or had planned to use as barricades. There was no sign of a fight. *Illusion? Sleep spell? Time-stop? Who the hell knows? It doesn't matter at the moment, anyway.* He slid his camera around the frame of the door leading deeper into the facility and identified a trio of wizards who guarded an intersection to the right. One faced in each direction, and there was finally definite audible signs of their quarry—glass shattered as what he imagined were evidence cases broken open to allow access. *At least we were able to separate and hide the most dangerous artifacts in there. Although if they have some way to detect them, that probably won't help for long.* He shook his head. *There are too many unknowns. It's past time I went with what I'm good at.*

He whispered, "Going noisy," and dialed his comms back to normal. The other team members spoke in short bursts as they emerged from cover to follow him. He barreled around the corner and raised his rifle to fire at eye level as he ran toward the invaders. The foe facing him yelped and ducked, and the others began to turn as a protective shield appeared to block the incoming rounds. It stopped none of the anti-magic bullets, but the enemies' reflexive flinches enabled them to evade the shots. Hank grinned when he located where the shimmer ended and launched himself into a slide on the linoleum floor, which he could now see was old but carefully polished, year after year. He careened into the first wizard and hooked his arm around the one to the side as he continued, and they all collided with the remaining man.

Whatever spells they might have tried to cast were lost in the impact, and the agent used the moment of surprise to his advantage. He thrust an elbow sideways into the face of a wizard and reversed the motion to deliver a punch to the forehead of the next. The third staggered to his feet but the ARES agent looped one foot behind his ankle and kicked his shin with the other. Bone cracked and the magic-user howled as he tumbled. Hank punched the man he'd stunned with the forehead blow and this time, caught him cleanly in the temple and rendered him unconscious. He scrambled to his feet and delivered a kick to the man with the damaged shin in the same moment that the witch appeared in the intersection.

She was visible only for an instant before a blast of force hurled him the length of the hallway. It stuck to him and shoved him ever faster until it hammered him into the far wall. His head cracked against the stone and his vision failed, replaced by blackness and white spots. It returned as a blurry mess a moment later, and he groaned at the discomfort of the unyielding floor beneath him. He managed to roll out of the way of the fireball that roared into the wall he'd impacted with but he could hardly put his thoughts together. With no time to spare, he snatched the healing potion at his belt and drained it in a single long draught. His back arched and he screamed in anger as the magic surged through him before he bounded to his feet and raced down the corridor toward the witch.

She'd been distracted in the interim by his allies, who fired at her from the same room he'd been in earlier. The woman used a fallen wizard to protect herself by levitating his body to absorb the incoming rounds. She failed to sense the large agent's approach until his fist met the place where her spine joined her skull. He didn't need to expend any of the magic that burned within him and a single blow was enough for her to sag and fall, out of the fight one way or the other. He spun as a hail of ice hissed down the hall toward him and stepped back to avoid it. A brief look had revealed a portal in the evidence room beyond and figures throwing boxes into it.

"Dammit, they're getting stuff out. I don't suppose any of you broke the rules on equipment, did you?"

Anik sounded sheepish but not particularly apologetic. "I might have a couple of extra grenades."

"Boom-boom kind?"

"The boomiest."

"Excellent. There are magicals defending the entrance. We'll lay cover down, you throw your explosives, and then we'll see what trouble we can cause." The others moved into position, Tony on the other side of the hallway that led to their targets while Anik readied himself for a run.

Starsky and Hutch remained a few steps behind, their weapons aimed. Hank nodded, stuck his rifle around the corner, and fired blindly. Tony did the same, and the demolitions expert dashed across the opening and hurled two canisters as he did so. They detonated an instant later, giving the wizards no time to react, and the large man rushed forward into the smoke and noise.

Calling them boom grenades had left the question of exactly what type they were open to interpretation. He'd thought of flash-bangs, but Anik apparently had other ideas. Shards of metal and flaming wreckage signaled his use of fragmentation and incendiary devices. The wizards had literally been shredded and beyond their remains, their comrades in the evidence room whipped their wands around to hurl two boxes into the portal. One stepped through after the cases, and the agent raced forward using his magic to accelerate toward the other.

When the man smirked and leapt sideways into the rift, Hank's body acted without any conscious direction, lunged in after him, and caught the escapee in a flying tackle. He braced for impact with the bars on the far side of the evidence cage, making sure the enemy was angled to take the brunt of the blow, but instead, slid across a concrete floor that hadn't been there a moment before, the wizard wrapped in his arms. He thrust the man's head against the hard surface as their momentum slowed and twisted onto his feet to face the room behind him.

The trip through the portal had deposited him in a garage of some kind. Boxes of various kinds and sizes were stacked in each direction. *Loot storage. It makes sense. And it could be anywhere since they can use magic to move it around.*

Three people in the room held wands and another three carried weapons, and they looked as surprised at his appearance as he felt. He drew his pistol, having emptied the rifle magazine at the wizards and failed to reload, and sprayed shots at the non-magicals. Their bulletproof vests kept them alive but the power of the unexpected attack still disabled them.

A blast of force hurled him to the side. He seized a post along his path, yanked himself around it, and used his magic to double his power as he swung himself toward the nearest wizard. The man tried to block him with one of the crates stolen from the evidence locker, which spewed its contents in all directions as it rocketed at his head. Hank caught it and used it as a battering ram to pound it into the wizard and propel him into the mage beside him. He grinned at the third, who was now within arm's reach, and pistoned a fist into his face before he could raise his wand in defense. He bound the fallen quickly and took stock of the situation.

"Glam, roll the police to my location but make sure one of our people arrives first. We'll want to take some of this stuff. Emphasize it as a police matter, use an unencrypted band, bring the media, all that garbage. I don't think there's any way they can know I'm more than merely a talented officer, but let's throw as much chaff in the air as possible to distract them."

He circled the room to break the boxes and assess what the enemy had acquired and stored in their bolt hole while Kayleigh gave him countdowns to Cara's arrival and that of the police. The number of magical artifacts was of real concern and he set them aside to "disappear" into ARES custody. More worrisome, however, was the sheer number of explosives and weapons they had gathered. Everything from machine guns to rocket launchers was stored in the cases and in a large enough volume that the gang probably rated as a medium-sized militia. *At least that equipment will go to the police or feds where it belongs.*

Cara arrived in an unmarked grey SUV and wore an illusion that made her look like one of the men in black from the movies. Together, they carried the single box into which he'd thrown all the magical items out of the garage and stored it in the car before they accelerated away and down the opposite side of the hill from the approaching media circus. The TV news helicopter might have been able to catch an image of them, but Kayleigh's drone blocked its progress with a false FAA message telling them that the airspace was temporarily closed. She'd laughed as she filled them in on the tactic as they left the scene.

The team's second in command dispelled the illusion and glanced at him. "Did you have fun?"

He sighed and cracked his knuckles. "You know it. I always love busting heads." His heart wasn't in it, though, and he knew she sensed it by her expression.

"What's the matter?"

Hank sighed again. "I get that the boss to some degree—and ARES overall—is about subtlety, and spycraft, and all that shit. But I think the time for that may be ending. We need to bash some heads in here."

She laughed. "I couldn't agree more. It might be difficult to convince the others, though. They're smarter than we are."

He chuckled, his momentary pessimism broken. "Well,

there's smart and then there's too smart for your own good. Fortunately, we're not at risk for that. But maybe they're suffering from it and need a smack upside the head to help them out."

She pressed on the accelerator. "That's an idea I can get behind, partner."

CHAPTER EIGHT

Diana looked at the armored mannequin with a sigh before she took the various pieces from the limbs. She put one foot up on the bench to strap her shin guard on and caught Nylotte's amused expression from where she sat in the comfortable chair that existed solely for the purpose of allowing the damned Dark Elf to bestow such looks upon her. The bunker—which now had no discernible remnant of Nehlan's time as owner except for the locked and warded door leading to the sealed portal room—was the preferred base to prepare for their next and hopefully last attempt to retrieve Fury, the remaining unclaimed piece of Rhazdon's Vengeance.

With one leg finished, she switched to the other. "So, do you think you've found it for sure this time?"

Her teacher laughed. "There's no way to know until we get there. Don't tell me you're getting frustrated already?"

She glared for several moments, then straightened and retrieved her forearm guard. "No, I'm not frustrated at all. I love traipsing through disgusting caverns filled with repulsive creatures, alive, dead, or in-between as the case may be. It's like a freaking vacation." The Drow's laughter displayed her complete lack of concern over Diana's ire, which was certainly par for the course. Once her arms were clad, she pulled on the chainmail-underlaid bullet-proof vest and secured the Velcro straps that would hold it tightly around her body. She carried her Ruger and Bowie knife in their holsters for backup, but otherwise, was prepared to depend solely on her magic. Somehow, it seemed appropriate given the task at hand. Her utility belt held the usual array of useful items in addition to two each of energy and healing potions.

Nylotte was in her own battle armor—black chainmail and leather that matched the shade of her skin perfectly. Her white hair was confined in a warrior's knot at the base of her skull. She carried knives at her hips and several vials on her belt as well. Despite her teacher's mirth, Diana could see the worry in the corners of her eyes and in the way she held her lips. The Dark Elf hadn't revealed what the frown at the end of their last training session was about, and she had decided not to ask. It didn't feel like she was the cause. In any case, there was no chance she could fear treachery from the Nylotte. It simply wasn't in the realm of possibility, given all that they'd been through, and the truth was that without the other woman's guidance, her ability to pursue the sword, much less retrieve it, would be zero.

The fact that she was kick-ass in battle was an extra bonus on top of all the things she really needed her for. Together, they were undoubtedly more than equal to any challenge they might face on the path to Fury. *Okay, maybe a little doubt. Only a tiny bit.*

The other woman rose and clapped sharply. "Are you finally ready? Do you take this long to prepare for a date? I would think your Bryant would get bored waiting."

She rolled her eyes. "First, he doesn't usually watch me get ready for a date and second, shut up, and third, you're simply jealous. Seeing Dreven again brought up some long-buried desires, didn't it?"

Her teacher's burst of laughter was exactly what she had intended. She grinned as the other woman shook her head. "You are such an idiot, Sheen. Honestly."

"You know you love me."

"Love and hate are divided by the thinnest of lines. Are you aware of that?"

Diana laughed. "You'd be so bored without me. Speaking of which, is it time to go yet? I'm getting tired of waiting on you, old woman."

The Drow growled and threw a portal at her.

She stumbled when the floor gave way to dirt and grass beneath her feet. She caught her balance as Nylotte stepped through and banished the rift. The twitch at the corners of her teacher's lips made the uncomfortable trip completely worth it. She looked around but saw only trees. They were in a clearing in a forest, and the trunks stretched high before branches jutted out from them to create a canopy above. The leaves were multicolored, from dark-yellow to a bright red on one tree, all green on the next, and all orange on a third. Together, they created a discordant atmosphere that set her teeth on edge.

She started at the sound of the other woman's voice. "This is the dark forest, a fair distance away from where your bunker is located. About a half-mile that way"—she gestured ahead of them—"is an old temple built by a cult from long, long ago. It has come up in several books as a potential place of power that Rhazdon was interested in, so it may very well be the location of the sword."

Diana nodded. "That sounds logical. Those trees won't make us insane or anything, will they?"

The Drow laughed. "The only sanity at risk here is mine, because of you. We won't be here long enough for them to affect us, and we're protected from the worst effects by the bark. It's the harvested wood or that of dead trees that are most dangerous."

"Great. I feel much better. Lead the way." Her teacher did exactly that, and the agent moved cautiously behind her and kept her attention on the path. It was rocky, crowded with the tops of boulders that needed climbing and scree that tried to dump her on her backside. The route wound as it climbed, and she was grateful it wasn't whatever passed for a rainy season in this part of Oriceran. The air was swollen with strange sounds—hisses and chirps that were completely unlike anything she'd experienced in the woods on Earth. Where sunlight filtered in, the atmosphere was pleasant and almost hopeful. In the spaces where the branches and leaves prevented illumination, the feeling was dark, foreboding, and decidedly lacking in hope. *One more place to cross off my vacation desti-*

nation list. Maybe a cruise. Yeah, like a month on a boat. That would be perfect.

An open area was visible ahead, and Nylotte slowed to let her catch up. Together, they crouched near the end of the path and looked into the clearing beyond it. The nearest item of note was a wicked wrought-iron fence, black and flawless, with nasty spikes protruding upward and to all sides at six-inch intervals. They shuffled a little closer so the trees no longer blocked their view, and it became apparent that the barrier circled the temple and the land around it, with the dark, gothic building located in the exact center. It was about the size of a medium-sized two-story house if you discounted the tall steeple that rose another couple of dozen feet to the sky from the peak of the roof.

The grass surrounding it was long and unmaintained but low enough that she could make out gravestones engraved with strange patterns all around the property. "Tell me there won't be zombies involved."

Nylotte's voice was dry and quiet. "There will not be zombies involved."

"Why don't I believe you?"

"A character flaw, I assume. Look there." She pointed at the windows, and Diana could make out dark figures moving inside the building, looking from this distance like variations on the grim reaper having a dinner party. "It's a cult of witches."

"A coven?"

Her companion shrugged. "You could call it that, although not every coven is a cult. These folks are, though. And no, before you ask, they aren't necromancers. Quite the opposite, in fact. They are thoroughly committed to returning bodies—and everything else—into the ash from which it supposedly arose."

Diana frowned. "So it's a cult of pyromaniacs?"

"That describes them fairly well, actually. I wouldn't depend on them only being able to use fire, but they certainly prefer it, according to what I could dig up about them."

"Heh. Dig up. Zombie joke. Nice. But seriously, how much will this suck?"

Nylotte sighed and twisted to face her. "It'll probably suck considerably. Unlike the other places, which weren't active as such, this one is a functioning temple and we have no way to know where the sword is. Once we're ready to reveal ourselves, I can cast a spell to help us track it, but these are witches with a significant skill level so I can't risk it before that moment."

"Okay, so we go up and say we want to join or something?"

Her teacher laughed. "The ritual for admission is to have yourself burned. If you heal enough to live, you get to stay."

A shudder ran through her. Burning was second only to being enveloped by shadow tentacles on her list of scariest nightmares.

"Girl Scout cookies?"

"Are you ever serious?"

"Not when I'm nervous. And I have to tell you, people who would willingly court death by burning simply to join a club make me *really* damn nervous."

"That's perfectly understandable. I don't like them

either. I think our best option is to circle and see if there's a back entrance to preserve secrecy as long as we can. If we can disable some of them silently, so much the better."

A grimace leapt unbidden to her lips. "Um, not to be overly goody-goody, but I'm not sure the fact that they're hiding a sword that's not actually ours is cause for a death sentence, you know?"

Nylotte frowned. "Have no worries on that matter. Most of their converts aren't taken willingly. The cult burns structures, traps their potential members inside, then helps those they deem worthy to recover from the experience. Invariably, their minds are twisted and broken in the process."

"Oh, okay, they're total assholes. Fair game then. Lead on, Kemosabe."

They crept along the perimeter of the black fence, staying low to avoid notice from those inside. As they followed a curved trajectory to the side of the building, they noticed more people moving about, silhouetted in the upstairs windows. All the light sources flickered and Diana came to the late realization that of course they only used open flame for lighting, feeling appropriately stupid for having taken so long to reach that conclusion. They continued their slow progress around the barrier, which remained unbroken until they reached the rear of the structure, which had three evenly spaced windows on the top story and two more surrounding a door on the ground level. More flickering and movement was visible through the windows.

Diana hissed. "How many of them are inside? It's like a clown car for witches or something."

Her teacher chuckled. "They do seem to prefer proximity, don't they? I've never been one to enjoy such things."

She thought about her own living arrangements and shrugged. "I guess it depends who you cohabit with. But these crazy people? No thanks."

"Being devout doesn't make them crazy."

"No, voluntarily burning themselves almost to death makes them crazy. And for the involuntary ones, not immediately killing the rest of them in revenge makes them crazy."

Nylotte pointed at the back door. "That's our way in. The witches upstairs are a concern, so we'll have to stay vigilant in case they come down to join the fun."

Diana shook her head. "I hope they do. They deserve to have their flames extinguished with extreme prejudice."

"I can't argue with that sentiment." The Drow nodded. "Let's get to it."

CHAPTER NINE

Nylotte studied the building for several minutes before she turned to the agent. "Up and Over." With a gesture, the other witch lifted them both from their feet and deposited them inside the fence. Diana felt a strange tickle as they crossed the boundary and assumed there was a defensive ward that the Dark Elf had dealt with. They landed and her teacher scuttled forward, remained low, and stopped beside the door. She flanked it on the opposite side, and both were careful to keep their heads below the line of sight from the windows.

The Drow made a gesture and snarled in disgust. "It's warded against magical entry." Diana slid the lockpick tool from her belt, recalled the first time she'd seen one used so long before by Bryant in DC, and raked the pins until the lock clicked. She eased the door open, peeked inside, and saw a corridor that led directly to the front door with what appeared to be a staircase going up on either side of it, based on the curved railings ahead. Openings were present near the far entrance, and another pair to both left and right at the back.

She moved aside to let the Dark Elf lead the way. As they crept forward, there was laughter from the room on the right and sounds of chopping and cooking from the left. Nylotte pointed to herself, then to the right, and they crossed to opposite sides of the hall. Her teacher gave signals to indicate they would meet in the same place afterward and drew her knives. The agent drew her own from its sheath when she realized her companion intended to avoid using magic for as long as possible.

The kitchen was large, dominated by a wood-fired stove and oven along the wall opposite the entry. To her left, attached to the back wall of the building, were shelves and a giant sink. To the right stood a broad metal object that was doubtless a cooler of some kind beside a doorway into the room beyond. The center of the space held a prep island she would have killed to have in her own house. It was topped by a thick wooden block, and a tall figure in a long black robe with a hood wielded a knife skillfully through an array of vegetables before her. She threw the good parts into an immense stew pot and the leavings into a rough metal bowl at her side. Her hands and the part of her face that Diana could sometimes see when she moved were covered with scars, which made her look far older than her straight posture and energetic chopping would suggest. She hummed a small tune as she worked.

Dammit. She couldn't justify killing the woman, even though leaving her alive would increase the danger. Instead, she waited until the witch turned away to gather more vegetables and hurried in behind her. She struck her

on the temple with the hilt of her knife and used her free
hand to cover her target's mouth. The witch struggled, and
it required two more blows to make her stop. Diana
lowered her gently to the floor and checked her pulse,
which was still present. She cut pieces of the woman's robe
off and used them to tie and gag her, then put her in the
corner near the cooler, hoping no one would come upon
her by accident. A quick shuffle took her back into the
hallway where her teacher waited. The other woman
nodded and pointed forward to indicate two cult members
in the room to the left and two in the room to the right.
They had barely begun to move where there was a sudden
noise from the area Nylotte had been responsible for.

They both stiffened and darted ahead, turned toward
their respective areas, and leapt inside. Diana found two
witches who were gathering their wands from where
they'd been seated at a dining table, and she used force
magic to thrust them both back against the walls before
they could secure the weapons. One fell, but the other
remained standing and charged forward to snatch a knife
from a low chest. She slashed wildly at the agent's head but
wasn't anywhere near good enough to be in her league.
Diana pivoted and struck the arm in a block with her left
fist, caught the woman's wrist with her right hand, and
pulled her into a left elbow strike that broke her nose and
felled her without even a squeak of protest. The other tried
to find her feet and Diana reached out with her telekinesis
and tipped the nearby china cabinet onto her. The
imposing item of furniture toppled with a satisfying eruption of breaking crockery and splintering wood.

She turned and met Nylotte in the hallway, the woman

apparently having dealt with her own targets. "What happened?"

The Dark Elf looked annoyed. "I didn't kill the ones in the first room. One of them managed to escape her gag."

The agent laughed. She couldn't help herself. "When we get back, I'll teach you the proper way to tie scumbags up, okay?"

Her companion pointed at the staircase. "Maybe we should focus on the here and now, hmm?"

She turned as two witches emerged onto the landing closest to her, followed seconds later by another two on the opposite side. Without waiting for her teacher, she sprinted up her flight of stairs and summoned a flame shield to intercept the cones of fire launched by the coven members. The force of their attack stole her momentum and she stopped halfway up, unable to press forward any farther. She was perfectly placed, however, to target Nylotte's opponents and threw a hail of icicles at them. Her partner did the same, and the attacks subsided as their enemies focused on defense. She reached the top of the staircase and released a force sphere that launched a witch into the next room, then pounded a kick into the closest opponent. The woman thudded into the wall and her wand fell from her hand, and Diana followed up with a round-house kick that effectively eliminated her from the fight.

The agent stalked into the bedroom into which the other woman had been flung and who now rummaged in a chest of drawers. "Oh no, you don't. No backup wand for you." She caught her with another force blast that flung her through the room's window to sprawl onto the grass below, narrowly missing two headstones. Diana looked through the broken pane and cringed at the narrow escape. "Let that be a lesson to you." She turned and walked away as she muttered, "I'm not sure what lesson that is, other than don't pick fights with people better at magic than you —which is probably everyone, because you're so damn stupid." She and Nylotte approached from opposite sides of the hallway and met in the middle.

"Well, that wasn't optimal," the Drow said acerbically.

"No. But at least it's done. What's next?"

"This." She gestured with her hands and colors glowed along her wrist, visible where her sleeve had ridden up a little to expose the flesh. When the motions stopped, her teacher looked irritated again. "It's nearby, but below. And not directly below. Which means…"

She let the sentence hang, and Diana groaned. "Which means there's some kind of damn disgusting cave or cavern or something down there that we have to deal with."

Her teacher nodded and they wandered through the first floor in search of the stairs leading down but failed to find them. Eventually, the agent gathered her wits and noticed that the living room had a suspiciously large open space that featured nothing but a rug. *How many movies have I seen with trapdoors by now? Rath would be appalled.* She moved the carpet aside to reveal the expected entrance to the space under the building.

The stairs to the lower level were steep and shallow, which required them to descend sideways. Nylotte generated a light sphere to guide their way, and they reached the end without incident. The basement proved to be as uninteresting as the rest of the house, and they prowled through the open space, looking for a clue to access what lay beyond the immediate area. The Drow focused on the wall that had been on the left as they'd entered and claimed to feel the pull of the sword most strongly from that direction. She muttered spells and incantations to reveal illusions, but to no avail. Diana searched for more mundane tricks and found a hidden door almost by accident, barely distinguished by a groove in the floor that had caught the toe of her boot as she moved past.

Predictably, the heavy stone barrier concealed a passage of hewn rock. She sighed, shook her head, and gestured her teacher forward. "After you, and once again, thank you for bringing us to such a lovely location." The door swung closed behind them as they advanced through the corridor and the dull thud made her jump.

Nylotte spoke into her mind without turning or stopping her progress through the hallway. *"This is a good sign. I can sense something ahead, and the tunnel is heading more or less in the right direction. I consider this a promising development indeed."* After another several minutes of walking, Diana was able to hear sounds from farther along the passage and crept closer to her partner. They stopped together when the corridor ended and a spacious cavern came into view, their perspective from somewhere near the top of it. The Drow lowered herself to her stomach, banished the light, and inched forward. The agent did the same and a few moments later, they reached the edge of a high platform that looked over a grand ritual chamber. A long curving stone staircase led down from the side nearest her.

A massive round table took pride of place below, and

one of the coven's witches was strapped to it, her cowl down to reveal her burned and hairless head and her arms and legs stretched seemingly as far as they could be and secured with metal bands. Around the edge of the object stood six other witches, alternating in position with the same number of men who presumably were wizards although there were no wands in sight, only knives—large, sharp, ornamental-looking knives. Several of the women were chanting, and Nylotte hissed at the sound. "Wretches. They still believe that sacrifice is necessary to transfer magical power. Their thinking is trapped somewhere in the last century."

Diana shook her head and whispered, "So blood ritual magic isn't a thing?"

Her teacher made a chopping gesture, clearly disgusted. "No. Blood can be used in magic but not to power magic. Their words are as nonsensical as their beliefs."

"So, should we break their party up?"

"Without question. The only variable is whether we do it before or after they kill the idiot on the table."

"Is she willing?"

"She seems to be. Look at her." Indeed, the woman did have a serene and almost blissful expression on her face and seemed entirely reconciled with what was to come. Of course, there was any number of assumptions wrapped up in that, including the biggie—that she knew what was to come.

Diana gestured at her. "I assume she's not the brightest bulb on the tree. It's surely possible she thinks it's all a play, right?" The Drow shrugged. "Okay, then, let's at least try to save her."

Her teacher pointed at the staircase. "Fine. You move that way. I'll attack them from up here and then we'll improvise."

She darted up and took the stairs at a run. *Improvising is what I do best.*

CHAPTER TEN

When Diana reached the bottom, Nylotte provided a distraction from above in the form of a shield that suddenly appeared over the table, followed immediately by a column of lightning that descended upon the gathered cultists. It was a great plan in theory but in retrospect, one or both of them should have noticed the wards etched into the stone floor that collected the magic and funneled it away from their enemies. Together, the magicals turned and raised their wands toward the platform to layer fire attacks until the stone itself began to glow and crack in the heat.

Fear spiked in the agent's mind and she pushed it aside. *I'm sure she's fine. Nylotte wouldn't let herself be killed at the hands of those she considers amateurs.* She theorized that the counterattack would have required them to deactivate the arcane protections and tested the premise with a series of force spheres thrown like baseballs. They grew in flight before they pounded into their targets, each of the three at an angle that would cause the recipient to stumble in the direction of one of their allies. The projectiles struck perfectly and half the enemies were momentarily disabled.

The others babbled unintelligible words and sprayed fire toward her. It was too much to catch with small bucklers, and she didn't want to find herself locked immobile inside a bubble like she'd been with Nylotte. Instead, she triggered her force magic to launch herself across the room. Subtle adjustments in mid-air accomplished by her telekinesis allowed her to land in a position where the cultists risked wounding one another if they tried the "burn everything" tactic again. She lashed out with a side kick. Her nearest adversary proved to be remarkably fragile and simply slammed into the table and crumpled with the sound of broken bones.

Diana ducked under a thin beam of fire, swept the attacker's legs out from under him, and rolled sideways to evade two more streaks of flame that intersected in the place she'd abandoned. She rose in a crouch with her bucklers extended, intercepted the next two attacks, and drew power from them to recharge her energy and maintain the defense. When a third fiery trail joined those two, she expanded the size of the shields and felt the magic begin to drain from her. The cultists she'd disabled began to push to their feet and she backed slowly away and circled toward the protection of one of the ornamental pillars that supported the rocky ceiling. She made the shields taller as the next series of attacks lanced in and saw with dismay that her foes were smart enough to spread apart to try to encircle her.

That, apparently, was the cue her partner had waited for. Nylotte materialized out of nowhere, standing near the bottom of the stairs Diana had used. She discharged lightning again and struck a third of the enemy with forked electricity that jumped from one to the next in what appeared to be a self-sustaining circle. Her teacher moved toward the second group while the initial targets twitched and lurched, and Diana flung herself toward the remaining foursome, holding a flaming barrier in front of her as she closed the distance between them.

The Dark Elf was the first to attack and shadow tentacles stretched hungrily to ensnare her adversaries. The cultists responded with fire swords to cut and slash at the translucent limbs, and a wry grin twisted Nylotte's lips. A quick gesture summoned ice under their feet, and they fell in an almost slapstick display of panicked flailing. Once they were down, she wound two in tentacles and covered another with enough ice to encase him. The last one rose and snarled a curse. She grinned at him. "Your group has always been insane, but I seem to recall that in the past, you were also competent. Apparently, that has changed."

His voice was hoarse and choked. "You have no idea of the torments that await you, evil one."

She laughed. "Evil? Little old me? Hardly. Now, burn." She flooded him with flame, and he shielded and counterattacked with the same. It was a classic image, the twin magical attacks meeting and fighting for dominance. Within moments, it was clear that Nylotte was the stronger of the two and her attack inched closer and closer to him. He lurched forward and stalled the advance for a moment before the inexorable progress resumed. When the flames finally surged over him, he screamed once in something that sounded like a mixture of pain and elation and fell silent. The Drow didn't cease her assault until only ash remained.

That battle barely registered in glimpses of sight and sound as Diana dealt with her own opponents. She ducked and wove through fire beams as she attacked, and at the end of the whirling and spinning, found herself surrounded by the four, who summoned flaming blades from the ends of their wands and lunged toward her. She marshaled her force power in an instant and released it in a circular wave to sweep her opponents off their feet. Without hesitation, she pressed forward and dispatched the first with a kick before he could recover, then disabled the second in the same way. The third and fourth decided a little distance was preferable and retaliated with wide cones of fire as they retreated. She held them off with a large flame shield and threw a low blast of ice beneath it. The disappearance of the incoming attacks heralded the success of her counter-attack, and she used force magic as they fell to bounce their heads off the stone floor and end their involvement.

She shook her head and turned to see Nylotte destroying the bindings holding the sacrificial victim to the table. The woman sat and lowered her hood, muttering. Diana leaned in to hear what she said and flinched away in time to avoid the wicked knife that licked out at her eyes. She reacted reflexively and her force magic thumped into the cultist to hurl her across the room and into a wide stone pillar. She collapsed bonelessly onto her face. The Drow laughed. "Of course. Like I said, they're insane and incompetent."

Diana shook her head. "Do you still think these are the guardians of the sword?"

Nylotte nodded. "More than ever. I sense it over there." She gestured toward the far wall, where they discovered—inevitably—another rough-hewn passage leading onward.

The agent groaned. "Is all of Oriceran like this?"

"No, there are many beautiful parts. And where our people are from is the most gorgeous of all."

"I'd like to see that sometime. Truly."

Her teacher made an approving sound. "Once we finish with these idiots and the ones on Earth, there will be more than enough time for you to explore your heritage. I would...enjoy showing it to you." The slight pause, as if it was an admission of an emotion she was uncomfortable with, gave Diana's spirit a boost.

"I would enjoy having you show it to me." She pointed at the passage. "For now, though, I guess you should lead on through there."

She scowled. "There are sure to be more idiots. But, as they say, there's no time like the present." She strode forward and summoned a ball of light to illuminate the path.

The corridor ended after a short distance and they emerged into an entirely unexpected room. It was an underground vault constructed of elegantly etched ebony blocks that marched upward in a spiral pattern to the dome above. The arrangement affected the eyes and made everything seem off-balance and strange. Illumination came from a ring of fire that burned in a groove directly before the courses of blocks began to narrow inward. There were no pillars and nothing else that seemed to support the towering ceiling above.

The floor of the room was made of a series of concentric rings that rose like stairs to a platform that filled at least half of the room's total space, making it about three times as large as Nylotte's training area. In the center stood a figure clad in black metal armor that was a combination of chainmail and well-placed plate, similar to her own but undoubtedly much heavier. It had a wide gorget at the throat and a helm resembling a stylized flame. A deep voice, clearly male but otherwise revealing nothing about his age or ability, emanated from within. "You have entered the Sanctuary of the Cinder. You will die for this offense."

Nylotte snorted. "If you're as inept as your followers out there, I don't think we have much to worry about. How about you hand over the sword and spare us the effort of taking it from you?"

He reached behind his back and drew a two-handed greatsword, the black blade inscribed with runes that glowed in silver. "This sword? Fury cannot be given, Drow. He must be won." He placed the weapon point down and rested his hands on the crosspiece of the large pommel. "Are you willing to challenge me? The battle is, of course, to your death."

The agent stepped forward and pointed at him. "Hey. Black Knight. Not her. Me. And it would definitely be better for you if you gave it up willingly. We've been through too damn much to leave here without that blade."

The man gestured with his hand and Nylotte was

brushed back from the platform. A barrier shimmered into place the instant her teacher crossed the threshold and sealed Diana in with him. She looked around. "So, how do we do this? Are there any rules?"

He grinned. "The strongest wins. The weakest dies. Those are the only rules that ever matter."

She shook her head. "Stupid rules for a stupid person. Being. Whatever." She pictured the scene with the sword wielder from *Raiders of the Lost Ark* and wished she had a pistol to do it right. *Oh well, magic will suffice. Let's get this nonsense over with.* She thrust her hands out and reached within for flame, intending to cook him inside his armor as a piece of poetic justice and be done with it in a single attack.

When it failed to materialize, her mouth opened in shock. When he laughed, she realized she was in trouble. Without magic, how could she defeat a seven-foot-tall iron monster with a sword almost as big as he was?

CHAPTER ELEVEN

The knight blurred into motion—far quicker than she'd anticipated he could—and whirled the sword into a powerful downward strike intended to end the battle instantly. She waited until the final second before she spun away, moving to her right since he'd seemed to favor his right hand slightly. *I gotta get every edge I can. Staying on his weak side is good. Maybe he'll get tired of trying to hit me and fall asleep.*

The next blow whipped across at head height, and she ducked under it and rolled immediately to the side as he stopped it and slashed back at a diagonal. *Okay, he won't tire anytime soon with that kind of strength. Plan B rejected.* She mentally cataloged the items in her utility belt as she dodged several follow-up attacks and came up with nothing that would be of use in the current circumstance. *Dammit.*

He paused his offensive flurry and let the sword rest on his shoulder. "Little girl, let's end this without undue pain. Stop running, and I'll take your head off with one blow. I promise, it will be as humane as a beheading can be. If you keep this up, you'll wind up getting chopped to pieces, which will hurt much, much more."

She pushed sweaty strands of hair off her forehead and took a few steps back. "Does that line ever work?"

The black knight laughed. "Not yet. But it's always worth trying. It takes forever for my followers to clean the blood up after."

He slid forward smoothly and delivered a stroke intended to split her up the middle, but she dodged and retreated out of the way of the follow-up horizontal strike. His words had inspired the beginnings of a plan, but she didn't love it and really hoped some other idea would miraculously appear. She backed closer to the translucent barrier and it sizzled as electricity flared to connect with her skin and make her shudder. She tried to pull from it to power her own spell and received a nasty shock for her trouble. The distraction almost cost her as the sword whipped in and narrowly missed her clavicle before she ducked and rolled away. He followed and she felt like an idiot as she fled in a circle, then cut across to try to create some distance between them.

He stopped and regarded her insolently, the weapon resting on the other shoulder now. "You have nothing. It is always those strong in magic who seek Rhazdon's leavings, and once without it, they cannot hope to defeat me." He lifted the sword into a high attack position. "You have been an interesting diversion, but it is time to bring this intrusion to a close. Once you are dead, I can return to my vigil and continue to increase the power of my followers in this world."

Okay. I guess it's all I have. She had carefully watched how he moved, noted the weak points where only chain-mail protected him, and identified a few places that might offer an opportunity. The cost of reaching them, though, had the potential to be devastating. She circled to her right to position herself perfectly and was rewarded with the one break she truly needed. His mighty strike intended to cleave her in two descended at an angle, rather than straight down. She skip-stepped to the right, raised her left arm with a quick prayer, and pivoted into her own attack.

The blade whipped downward and struck the armor plate strapped to her left forearm. If he'd chopped verti-cally, it probably would have overcome the protection and cut her arm in half, but the angle caused it to bite the metal and skid off. The impact fractured the bone and she bit down on a scream when she forced the damaged limb to do its job and grasp his wrist. She finished her pivot and rammed her right palm into his elbow, just above the defensive spike on the guard. The joint broke under her attack, and he bellowed in anger as she spun and stumbled away, cradling her arm. She yanked a healing flask from her belt and drank it quickly, hoping against hope that whatever blocked her magic wouldn't work against it, too. The vaguest of tingles whispered through her body and the injury throbbed a little less painfully, but that was the only change. She threw the empty container aside with a curse.

It was nothing compared to the stream of vile epithets that erupted from the dark knight's mouth, however. His struggles to lift his greatsword one-handed were a source of solid amusement for her until finally, he stood tall and raised it, carefully maintaining the weapon's balance as he stalked slowly toward her. His stroke was awkward and she dodged it easily. The blood seeping from his broken joint brought a relieved smile to her face. Based on the way he swung the blade and flailed rather than struck precisely, he seemed to know that he was losing any opportunity he had to defeat her. He launched a kick when she was close, but his heavy armor slowed him and she skipped away without difficulty.

She gestured at the sword. "Lay it down now, and we'll call this done. I'll take the weapon and you can stay here and play with whatever idiots are stupid enough to commit to your cause."

He snarled and lunged at her, swinging the massive blade wildly. When she saw the opening, her body moved before her mind even registered it. Instead of spinning to the outside, she spun inward toward him. Her torso twisted to avoid the blade, and she levered her back under him, drove up with her legs, and tilted to one side. The impact against his core lifted him enough to break his balance, and he began to topple to the side. She slid out from under the giant man, clawed at his hand, and punched his wrist with a tight fist. He fell to the left and the sword to the right. She raced to it and scooped it up, then turned to find him staggering to his feet and clutching his broken elbow. The arm beneath it was crooked, and she realized he must have landed on it.

His voice was filled with rage and agony. "Put my sword down, you insolent gnat."

She'd had enough. To have the object of their search finally in her grasp should have felt like a victory. Instead, it was an exhausting end to the effort. All she wanted was to rest. *For a month. Only a month.* "I'm leaving and I'm taking this with me. Drop the shield."

He shook his head. "I explained the rules. Only death serves."

"This is your last chance."

"Give me the sword, woman."

"Okay, you asked for it." She screamed in rage and drove forward to thrust it into his chest. When the blade pierced him, the body within the armor transformed into a pillar of flame and she scrambled away from it and fell. In moments, it was gone and the hot and smoking remnants of his armor lay scattered on the dais. Nylotte stepped to her side. Her teacher helped her to her feet without a word and opened a portal to the bunker's bedroom. Diana stumbled as she passed through, then lost consciousness as the Drow laid her on the bed. The last thing she heard was the Dark Elf's pride-filled voice. "Well done, Diana. Well done."

CHAPTER TWELVE

Kayleigh waved at the bartender to order another round. The Irish Pub was her other favorite spot on the city's South Side, and she'd decided it was time to share it with Deacon, who professed to be a fan of Manchester United. The bar opened early for those who wanted to gather and watch the game, and the rest of the main street was quiet on a Sunday morning so it was a perfect setting. With a flawless slide, a second pint of Strongbow arrived in front of her and a Guinness was set reverentially in front of her partner. A plowman's lunch plate sat on the top of the wooden bar between them, almost half already gone.

A cheer sounded as a goal was scored. Deacon apparently remembered he wasn't there alone and turned toward her. "So, are you enjoying the game?"

She shrugged. "Team sports kind of aren't my thing. Give me a good one-on-one matchup any day."

"Sacrilege."

Kayleigh laughed and gestured at the crowd. "Don't let them know my secret. They seem rowdy."

He nodded. "Unbridled enthusiasm is a requirement to be a football fan." He stared at her for a moment and sighed. "Okay, spill it."

His partner took a long, delaying sip to order her thoughts. "I've been thinking about the R-gang." *Okay, it's not a complex code, but there's no need to talk openly either among these drunken fans. You never know who might be around.*

He nodded and his attention focused more intently on her as he turned his back to the screens. "Everyone is doing all they can where they are concerned. I'm sure they'll be taken care of."

She shook her head. "I'm not doing all I can. Well, we're not since I'll need your help to do the thing I'm thinking of."

"Okay, walk me through it."

"We have the watchers, which give us a good surveillance foundation. We can tap the PD drones as well so I feel like that's all covered. As long as you're running traps and watches set up on the gang's email and stuff."

"I do, in a geofence around the storage place." He didn't say warehouse, but she knew he meant the Remembrance's base of operations. "When they're outside there, we don't have much other than the ones Face has tagged." They'd provided Sloan with stickers to attach to electronic devices when the opportunity presented itself. They looked like harmless pranks but allowed for tracking and intercepts. The under-cover agent had managed to apply a few of them thus far.

"Right, so that part is reasonably under control. Then we have the stun ones." Their own fleet of stun drones now numbered a dozen, with an additional two offline for maintenance at any given moment. The use of off-the-shelf parts had allowed them to ramp up quickly. "Ours are good, and those the PD inherited from when the Cube was in place are there to supplement."

He nodded again. The downtown precinct had anywhere from eight to sixteen weaponized drones available depending on tasking and state of repair. ARES had direct access to them by arrangement with the city and indirect access through a small box she and Deacon had installed in each when they took them for "test runs." Should the police decide not to share—or worse, conclude that BAM Pittsburgh was a target for some reason—they'd find the devices unwilling to obey problematic instructions. That particular operation had caused a little conflict for Kayleigh's sense of right and wrong but ultimately, it was merely a backup plan against someone else choosing to behave unethically. "Okay, so, that's the foundation. But what has you tweaked?"

"I had an idea."

"You have many ideas. You're like an idea machine."

"Yeah, but this one is a little more out there than usual. I was laying in the back yard looking at the stars last night when I saw a strange winking, and then some more lights making the same pattern. Alfred tracked them, and it turns out the Air National Guard base out at the airport has some new toys."

Deacon frowned. "What kind of new toys."

"Serious ones." She leaned forward so no one would overhear. "Lethal ones."

"For urban use?"

Kayleigh shook her head. "I doubt it, but that's something you should look into, computer wizard. I'm more concerned with how we'll deal with them, on two levels. First, if there was a call to use them against us or if the enemy managed to take control of them, we need to plan a defense. That much is obvious. But...well, we might also want to see if we could maybe...uh, hijack them. If we needed to."

A look of shock grew on his face. "Are you serious?"

"I know. It's totally not like me, right? It's only that everything seems so dangerous lately and we don't have the slightest clue what's going on half of the time. What if they suddenly decide to start killing people indiscriminately? That woman in charge of the group is legitimately crazy. I don't think we can have these weapons in our backyard and not prepare plans to take them over and use them if the situation called for it."

"We'd need to agree on what that situation was if I'm going to be any part of this."

She nodded. "Exactly what I was thinking. You and me —only you and me. We find out how to do it, we do what needs to be done to make it possible, and only ever mention it to anyone else if we agree to do so. We don't ask permission and we don't allow anyone to order us."

He looked into his drink. "That's kind of professionally dangerous."

"Everything we do is dangerous." She snorted. "The key element is we have to be able to live with ourselves. And I don't think I could do that if someone else held the keys to that option."

He slapped the bar. "Okay, I'm in. Let's do it." A loud cheer filled the room, and they were both startled, then realized that the home team had won the game.

Right. Let's do it.

The alert that the sensors inside the Remembrance witch's apartment had gone active came as she entered the house. Rath and Diana were out training together—a rare occurrence these days—so she headed to the basement to listen in. A muttered command to Alfred switched her gaming setup to work mode and changed the lighting, the sources for the monitors, and her keyboard layouts. By the time she was seated, the captured video and audio streamed into the high-end displays and the speakers.

It was always weird peering into Sarah's life like this. Kayleigh had no voyeuristic tendencies whatsoever, given her feelings about the importance of privacy, so watching as Alfred displayed the woman lying down and rearranging her furniture felt very unnatural. A clock in the corner indicated the feed was running on a 173-second delay, the duration it had taken her to get into position. The witch must have been eager to commune with whoever it was she talked to since she hadn't changed, made food, or done any of the things normal people did when they came home.

Okay, I didn't do any of those things either, but I never claimed to be normal.

The tech retrieved a herbal energy drink from the

mini-fridge, popped the top, and took a large sip as Sarah began to talk. It was also extremely weird to hear only one side of the conversation and have to try to piece together the other part. On several occasions, she and Deacon had spent an occasional giddy hour replaying the feeds and putting their own hilarious comments in place of whoever was chatting with the witch. Fortunately, only the two of them plus Alfred knew of it, and they'd all promised never to tell.

She sounded fearful. "Yes, you are correct. It was a dismal failure yet again. Everything went according to plan, but one police officer had magic and used it to wreck the escape." She paused as if listening. "No, I'm not sure why he wasn't eliminated with the others on the way in. My people tell me they killed everyone they saw. Maybe he used his power to hide. But if so, they should have detected it. No, I honestly don't know."

Sarah's body—wearing a black dress that had gone slightly grey with repeated washing and her stringy hair in need of a wash—twitched on the camera as Kayleigh waited for the next comments. She was already typing a summary of the discussion in one window and spinning up the watchers throughout the city in another in case there was something revelatory on the way.

"As I mentioned before, I have long thought there was someone working against us from the inside. I guess it was wishful thinking to assume it was Marcus and that it would stop once he was gone." After a pause, she continued with palpable anger in her voice. "No, I don't think it was random. I think one of the human scumbags is a traitor." Her head tilted as she scowled in silence. "There are maybe thirty who have been with the group since the beginning. Too many to simply kill outright, unfortunately."

Kayleigh pressed the buttons to send the recording to Diana. The threat against Sloan was clear and hopefully, once she listened to the feed, she'd find a way to get him cover—or, even better, pull him out of the gang.

The witch laughed, and it was an evil, unhinged sound. "Oh yes, I think I can spin together a trap that even the cleverest mouse wouldn't be able to resist and won't be able to escape. Consider it done." The tech tapped more buttons and flagged the recording to Diana as an urgent priority. The boss's AI would interrupt if it were possible to do so to draw her attention to the message.

On the screen, Sarah waved a hand in the air. "That other thing is all taken care of. The word is out, and there are apparently a number of people vying for the prize. Setting the bounties that high had the result we intended. Maybe it'll even pay off in the end." She laughed again. "The underling has already weathered one attack and more are sure to come. The leader should face her own imminently." There was a pause, and she sounded defensive when she spoke again. "No, we don't really control the timing. We merely put the contract out and they bring back the proof and get paid. They're not employees or anything."

The witch screamed, and her body thrashed and fell off the couch onto the floor. Kayleigh tapped a command to zoom in on her face and saw that it was bloodless and looked frozen in fear. It took several seconds for the enemy leader to gather her wits before she climbed to her feet and muttered, "I hate it when she does that." She staggered toward her bedroom, looking tired, and the tech returned the systems to automatic surveillance.

She leaned back in her chair and rubbed her eyes while stress gathered like a steel ball in her stomach. The generalized danger, the specific contracts that had been put out on Cara and Diana, the threat to Sloan, and the plan to compromise the National Guard drones all warred within her for the position of chief worry. She checked the clock, saw that it was far too early to find a decent online matchup, and turned to her computer with a sigh. *I can start working on the code for the drones and wait for the boss to tell me what to do about Sloan. It's not everything, but it's something.*

CHAPTER THIRTEEN

Diana stepped through the portal to her old house and immediately noticed that Lisa had repainted. She was about to say something snarky when her best friend forever pulled her into a hug that crushed the breath out of her. When she managed to wiggle out and speak, the excitement in Lisa's eyes was too genuine to dent with her sarcasm, so she told the truth. "It looks great. When did you find the time to do this?"

Lisa grinned. "I took a vacation. Work's a little slow at the moment."

"Still?"

"Yeah. I don't get it. But, you know, whatever. Let me show you the rest!" She didn't resist as the other woman dragged her through the house, showing her all the improvements she'd made. Finally, laughing, she inter-rupted the tour.

"I have to go meet with some fancy people."

"That explains the outfit. It's so not you."

The agent put her hand over her heart. "Ouch. Cruel.

Cruel and heartless." She'd adopted a different style for the day, mainly to surprise Bryant, who she saw far too infrequently of late. The stylish spy boots were still part of the arrangement, but a long skirt and matching jacket, plus a bright red blouse, finished the ensemble. Her hair, nails, and makeup received extra attention too, and she was, she thought, looking extremely professional.

Her friend laughed. "I'm kidding. You look great. For a lawyer."

She shook her head. "Shut up, or I'll stab you."

Lisa's reply was interrupted by a knock on the door, and she opened it so Bryant could enter. He had one glimpse of Diana and uttered a comical wolf whistle, which made all three of them break into laughter before he sobered quickly as he looked at his watch. "We're running late. Gotta go. Sorry to be rude."

He summoned a portal and signaled for Diana to lead. She stepped through into a standard institutional corridor. Bryant led the way through the twists and turns until they arrived at Finley's office. They entered through the outer door and were confronted by a thin, perfectly dressed secretary. He stood, smiled at them, and asked, "Bates and Sheen?" Bryant nodded, and the man gestured at the chairs against one wall. "The senator will be with you in a couple of minutes." He sat again and slipped on a headset, then began talking to someone they couldn't hear.

She leaned over to speak quietly to her boyfriend. "Is this normal? Should we be worried?"

He also kept his voice low. "There's no danger from Finley. I guess it's possible he has a guest in there who might concern us, but I think we're okay."

Her concerns vanished as the man himself appeared to escort them into his otherwise empty office. He veered toward the coffee machine and gave her time to examine the space. The carpet was thick and deep-blue, and the expected flags of the United States and his home state were in the two corners behind the desk. One wall was filled with bookshelves, and the other featured the long coffee-holding credenza, with storage below and a painting representing a scene from the revolutionary war above. Diffuse light was cast from beneath a molding that ran along the upper part of the wall and the illumination bounced off the flat white ceiling to give the whole area a warm feel.

The senator set mugs before them on his dark wooden desk and circled to take his own seat, a high-backed leather office chair. Piles of paper were arrayed in neat rectangles across the surface, and he moved the page he'd been working on to the side. He closed the lid of the nearby laptop and slid it away as well, then looked at his guests. "Thanks for coming."

They nodded and Bryant asked, "What's up? It was a surprise to hear that you wanted to meet with both of us."

"I have some bad news. We've been following the trails you provided and have discovered that all the members of the oversight committee, except for the vice president, have been compromised to some degree. Even me."

Diana blinked at the shocking information. "How?"

Finley shrugged. "The investigators aren't sure. They're operating under the assumption it's a traitor within since that's the worst-case scenario, but there are other reasonable explanations as well. It could simply be a really good virus but the search will expand to our homes. You can expect that they'll look at you all next."

She shook her head. "No way am I letting them into my systems. That will never happen."

Bryant nodded. "I have to agree. For all we know, they're the ones doing the compromising."

The man spread his hands wide in a gesture of helplessness. "Which is exactly why I called you here. I'd expected things would be moving toward the 'improvement' side of the continuum by now but instead, they're spiraling toward the 'seriously messed up' part." He sighed and took a large sip of his coffee, then retrieved a device she recognized from his desk. He placed the flat black square on the wooden surface and pressed the button to activate the signal jammer. "I can't leave this on too long or they'll think it's deliberate rather than an error." He chuckled. "You need to check in with Taggart. I gave him a heads-up when I visited him. He'll tell you the rest. We've planned for this but had hoped never to use the plan." He turned the box off and his tone shifted and became harsh. "So, you'll be required to give them full access, whether you approve or not. Remember, ARES is under governmental oversight for a reason. If you don't like it, you can feel free to submit your resignations. Do you understand?"

They put on appropriately cowed expressions and nodded. Bryant said, "Yes, Senator, we understand completely. Thank you for your time."

He led her from the office and they took the long way out of the building onto the plaza. Once outside, he turned and pulled her into a hug and whispered into her ear. "You and I are almost certainly under surveillance, individually and together. I have a low-level jammer on but keep it neutral until we're with Taggart." He released her, plucked his phone from his inside jacket pocket, and summoned a car. They wandered arm in arm like tourists while they waited, looking at the many plaques and arrangements of greenery that decorated the wide space. Finally, the expected SUV rolled up to the curb and they stepped in for the ride to the hospital.

Carson Taggart sat in a large recliner, which was far better and more comfortable overall than where he'd spent his time while in the coma. He rose quickly but unsteadily to greet them both with handshakes before he fell heavily in his seat. "It's so nice of you both to come. Is this a social visit?" His lopsided grin revealed that he was quite aware of the reason for their presence in his hospital room. They sat on the bed and faced him.

Bryant laughed. "You try to get out, but they keep pulling you back in, right, boss?"

The older man shook his head. "Like hell, Bates. I'm only here to teach you whippersnappers a thing or two." He gestured, and Bryant retrieved his jammer and set it on the low table beside the man's chair. It pulsed with a green light to confirm it was active. Taggart's demeanor changed, and he leaned forward with an energy she hadn't expected from him. "Okay, we don't have all that long before someone interrupts us for one thing or another, I imagine, so let's get going." He cleared his throat. "We knew from the beginning that the oversight committee could prove to be a problem, and while we wanted that connection with the government, we feared the possibility that politics might interfere with our mission. So Finley and I, and several others, came up with a backup plan."

"Project Adonis, right?" Bryant interrupted.

The older man laughed. "Yes. We love Greek mythology in our particular corner of the government, it seems. Anyway, the backup plan was to be invoked only under a few circumstances, but one of them was the discovery of traitors on the oversight committee or in the political chain of command that interfaces with us."

Diana shook her head. "Well, we certainly have that. Finley said that it's essentially ubiquitous—the penetration of our political side."

He nodded. "That's more or less how we envisioned it might happen, actually. Did he tell you that the vice president has overridden his selections for new members and is placing his own choices in there?"

Bryant made a choking sound. "What the hell?"

Taggart chuckled darkly. "Exactly. So, what we have here is a situation where the organization itself could be compromised. That can't be allowed to happen, lest our enemies manage to turn it to their advantage."

She drummed her fingers on her arm. "Okay, what's the plan, then?"

"You get ready to move on a moment's notice. Everything that's essential lives in crates, trucks, or other easily transportable items. When the time comes, if the situation reaches a breaking point, you vanish to a new central location and keep doing what you're doing."

Diana frowned. "We leave whatever we can't carry behind and go into hiding?"

He nodded but didn't speak. Silence reigned in the room for almost a full minute before Bryant broke it. "That's...a big ask."

The man sighed. "Yes. I know. There's a reason ARES agents tend to be unmarried and generally disconnected from things outside of their jobs. We never wanted to create a situation where someone would have to choose between competing loyalties."

She cursed. "I get it. And while it makes sense—total sense—it still sucks."

Both men nodded. Bryant asked, "Can you give us more details?"

"Everything but the timing and the destination."

"Okay, let's get to it before some handsome nurse comes in to offer you a sponge bath." The laughter at the joke was strained and almost painful but it was there. Which was something, at least.

Diana and Bryant had planned a romantic night out but the news from Finley and Taggart had killed their enthusiasm, so they simply went to her hotel instead. They lay together on the bed, fully clothed, and stared at the ceiling.

Neither spoke for some time but finally, Diana said, "You know, it could be worse. We'd be in the same location for once, anyway."

He laughed. "Are you asking me to cohabitate, Sheen?"

She slapped him with the back of her hand. "Don't be a jerk."

"I'm a slave to my instincts, you know that." He turned serious. "It's true. It could be much worse. Secrecy would keep us all safe from the garbage you're dealing with and protect us from the kind of stuff that happened in Buffalo and Hartford." He shook his head. "But, man, we'd give up all semblance of a normal life. I'm not sure my people signed on to be round-the-clock soldiers for ARES."

"Maybe we need to give everyone an opportunity to opt-out now before things reach the point of no return."

"Which risks giving the whole operation away." He sighed. "I know it's the right thing to do but let's not go overboard yet. If we're lucky, it could be that we can get out of this mess without ever needing to activate Adonis."

She shifted to lay alongside him and rested the back of her head on his shoulder. "And, yes, if we lived in the same city, I'd be willing to let you move in with me. On a trial basis. Assuming Rath approved."

He laughed. "I'll always be second to the troll, is that it?"

"Of course. We're partners for life, he and I."

He closed his eyes and ran his fingers through her hair. "I wouldn't have it any other way."

CHAPTER FOURTEEN

Rath was in his favorite place on Earth—out in the sun with his hands grasped around Max's collar while the dog ran and jumped joyfully through the people-filled streets. Technically, they were on patrol and the Borzoi's small saddlebags were packed with essential gear, but it was as much about being together as it was about looking for trouble. The team had already crossed the boundary from their home neighborhood into the area where the universities were, and numerous students outside out in the pleasant weather provided Max with enthusiastic attention and the troll with surprised compliments when they noticed him.

Once upon a time, he'd worried about how the people on this planet would treat him. By and large, though, experience had shown that they were extraordinarily accepting, aside from a few scumbags here and there. He didn't feel the need to hide, even at his smallest size. And, if someone threatened him enough to cause him to grow to his biggest version, they would probably be the ones in trouble.

He and Diana had spent more time together lately, sometimes training and sometimes watching movies late at night. It was perfect in a soul-filling kind of way. When she was unhappy, he was unhappy, so it was good that her mood had taken a turn for the better, especially after her successful retrieval of the sword. She had been a little bummed after the trip to Washington, but they'd spent the evening playing board games and her attitude had improved again. All it had required was giving their roommate a harsh defeat in Catan to accomplish it.

When his comms unit pulsed to indicate an incoming message, he gave the dog the signal to stop so he could listen to it without distraction. The electronic voice he'd come to associate with Amadeo crackled to life. Kayleigh had decided not to try to lock the assassin out of the comms but had instead adjusted everyone else's links to broadcast on a different channel. She'd set the old frequency to receive-only for everyone but the troll so the man wouldn't know they were all able to hear him. Rath could send on both the old and the new channels. The mysterious voice spoke quickly. "Your friend with the antique shop is in danger. You should get there immediately."

He yelled for Max to run, and the dog lurched into motion. Emanuel's store was only a few blocks away, and fear for the older man's safety coursed through him. He crouched low as his mount surged beneath him, and they covered the distance quickly. On the way, he instructed Gwen to summon the police, even though he knew they wouldn't make it there before he would. He mentally reviewed the locations of his gear in the bags and fretted as they bounded along the final block. The screen door hung from its hinges, and the sight made him instantly angry. He slipped off Max's back, grew to his three-foot size, and yanked his knives and batons from the dog's satchels. Kayleigh had added magic deflectors to the knife vest, so he had some defense against the witches or wizards he assumed would be inside.

"Max, follow. Free to bite."

He pushed the damaged door aside, slipped through, and heard loud voices from upstairs where the artifacts were. Another noise ahead indicated that someone was in the kitchen. He definitely didn't want to get caught from behind, so that one had to go first. He pointed to the base of the stairs and ordered, "Max, guard." The dog crouched out of sight but his posture suggested he was ready to make any intruder who might come down the staircase very unhappy. Rath crept down the hallway toward the source of the sound and darted hasty glances to the right as he passed doorways to ensure no enemies were lying in wait.

When he arrived in the entrance to the kitchen, he froze and studied a man dressed in dirty camouflage who a carried gun at his hip and faced the open refrigerator while he tilted a bottle of beer to his mouth. The invasiveness of the gesture irritated the troll, and he growled as he ran toward the offender. His target turned, his eyes filled with surprise and fear, and collapsed when the shock batons snapped at him. The bottle fell in his lap and the remaining liquid poured over him. *Risky move. Lucky break. Bad Rath. No, Totally worth it.* Thinking about Deadpool returned him to the right state of mind, and he hurried to the stairs and gestured for Max to follow him up.

They crept along the hallway and identified two strange men in the main area with Manny, one waving a wand and the other holding a pistol aimed at the old man. His friend looked like he'd been punched more than once, probably in an effort to force him to reveal where the artifacts were. It appeared that the intruders were in no hurry, which was a good sign and meant the rescuers had time as well. Rath suppressed his growl, not ready to let the invaders know he was there. Dog and troll moved to the next room and found one more with a rifle strap slung over his back. The troll pointed at Max and then at the enemy, and the dog's eyes indicated his understanding.

Rath retraced his steps to the entrance to the first room and readied himself. He was a moment away from launching his attack when two things happened. First, the thug with the pistol raised it as if to strike Manny, which made the older man flinch. That made his friend look toward the door, and his mouth opened in surprise. Both enemies immediately turned toward the troll and his element of surprise vanished as if it never existed at all. *Okay, we'll do it the fun way.*

His first priority was to protect Emanuel. He darted forward and slashed with his baton at the hand holding the gun, and the weapon spun free. An attack from the mage caught him, but his deflectors flared and absorbed the magic energy. There was no cracking sound, so he assumed he would be protected from at least one more attack. Making sure he remained between the wizard and the innocent human in the room, the troll sidestepped the rifleman to get a better angle and delivered four blows in rapid succession with his batons—shin, opposite knee, thigh, and a stab into the man's groin to finish the cycle. The stun blast discharged, the man yelped, and he stumbled back before he fell.

The mage launched another onslaught and Rath's deflectors surrendered beneath it. They grounded most of the lightning but it left his hair sticking up on end in every direction. He dropped his batons and cross-drew two knives to hurl them at his assailant. The wizard waved his wand and they changed trajectories and twisted to target Manny. The troll's eyes widened in panic as he flung himself into their path. His airborne blades caught the ones still sheathed along his ribs when he blocked their flight. He landed, vaulted up again to dodge the shadow bolt his foe delivered, and thrust off the wall and down toward the mage with a roundhouse punch. The man had no time for a magic solution, but he was light on his feet and managed to evade the fist.

As Rath recovered his balance from the missed blow, he realized Max was barking his head off and boots pounded noisily in the hallway. *Dang. Reinforcements. And I didn't hear sirens, so they're probably not on my side.* The wizard grinned, and his diminutive opponent did the only thing he could think of. He yelled, "Max, run!" and began to grow. He gathered his friend in one arm and snagged his vest as the Velcro parted and it fell away, then raced to the window. Glass shattered and wood splintered as he leapt through it. He landed on the soft grass of the backyard already running and at his full height. The dog joined him moments later, growling his frustration loudly to the world. Honestly, the troll felt like doing the same.

Once they reached a safe position where any oncoming threats would be easily visible, he lowered the man to the ground, shrank to his preferred size, and donned the vest again. Manny was unsteady on his feet and put a hand on his rescuer's shoulder to keep himself upright. "Thank you, my friend. That was terrifying."

Rath nodded. "Scumbags abound."

He gave something between a cough and a laugh. "I managed not to give up the secret of the illusion hiding the artifacts, but I assume they'll be able to discover it without me. I think..." He paused and shuddered. "I think they wanted to hurt me for its own sake, regardless of the information I was hiding."

"Sounds like them. Total jerks." He squinted at the building they'd fled, tried to make out a smudge that had appeared near it, and sighed. "House burning."

Manny uttered a sound of despair and hung his head for several moments. The troll didn't know what to say, so he put his hand atop the man's where it rested on his shoulder. Finally, with a dark laugh, the antique collector raised his chin to its normal confident position. "Ah, well. They're only things. What's important is that you rescued me and none of us were seriously hurt." A note of his familiar humor entered his voice. "And I'll have to work all the harder to find new treasures to replace the old ones. Plus, the insurance will be nice."

Rath laughed, and his friend joined him. The blaze intensified until they could see actual flames in addition to the smoke. Gwen spoke in his headphones. "Police on the scene, fire department two minutes out."

"Good work. Call Professor Charlotte to pick Manny up."

"Will do."

The man gave his shoulder a squeeze before he removed his hand. "Thank you again, my friend."

He shook his head. "My idea to give you artifacts. My fault."

Manny laughed and shook his head. "Oh, no, you simply added a little additional value. It was an open secret that I coveted and collected artifacts. I'm sure they've known about my place since forever but had bigger fish to fry before they got around to little old me." He paused to watch the house blaze for a few moments, then added, "That's one of the reasons we ancient people banded together. With our collective interests, it was inevitable that someone bad would notice."

Rath shrugged. "Still."

"Well, there's one way you can make it up to me if you still feel guilty."

The troll looked at him. "Name it."

"Get me one of those radios so I can contact you if there's trouble. How did you know to come help me, anyway?"

He grinned. "Got a tip. Lucky. And yes, radios for all of you." He turned and peered into the distance, where the cathedral in the center of the university towered above all the buildings nearby. It was time to get moving. "Stay safe. See you soon."

With his gear safely stowed on Max, he shrank and activated his tiny comms for the headset. As the dog ran toward their destination, he gave orders to the AI. "Gwen, ask Kayleigh for radios. Also, send drone with flight suit to top of Cathedral. We need to track them before they get away, so deploy nearby watchers."

"Got it."

You may think you've won, but the game's only begun. Scumbags. No one threatens my friends.

CHAPTER FIFTEEN

E ven in the summer, the lobby of the cathedral tower was busy with students, teachers, and tourists all going about their own tasks. No one took particular notice of the dog or the troll riding him, and they slipped into the elevator with no problem. The student ID Professor Charlotte had provided for him allowed them access to the top floors beyond the normal public areas, and he'd identified a window he could use to get outside some time before. When the doors opened, he shifted to his three-foot size, retrieved his headphones and goggles, and gave the Borzoi a pat goodbye. Max had made it home on his own countless times before and was properly tagged so he wouldn't be mistaken for a stray.

Rath crossed through the darkened hallways and used his acrobatic skills to take him up through a transom window that stood above a locked classroom door. A window on the far wall led out to a ledge that ran around the building, and he walked carefully along it to a corner where the stonework provided a path upward. After another story or two of climbing, he was on the roof at the pinnacle of the cathedral, no larger than a small bedroom. His crate of gear rested nearby, deposited by one of three customized watcher drones that were distributed at several equidistant points in the city. When he pressed his palm against the scanner, the locks clicked open.

He lifted the lid and removed his gear. First was the modified knife vest—complete with anti-magic deflectors —that sacrificed two blades to allow for the remainder of his flight suit to fit. He pulled the straps tight and checked that the throwing knives were ready to be drawn. Next, the armored pads at shins, thighs, forearms, and upper arms were followed by his utility belt and batons. Finally, he donned the harness that linked into the belt and wound around his chest with the wing box attached. He wiggled it into place quickly, a result of long practice, before he tugged his goggles on. Immediately, information began to fill them. A map appeared in overlay with pulsing red dots and two white ones.

"What's the situation, Gwen?" He closed and locked the case.

"White dots are Emanuel and Charlotte, who have separated—presumably having noticed they were being followed. Red dots are identified enemies." Rath noted that the scarlet circles seemed to be following the pale ones and grimaced. There were two criminals in pursuit of each of his friends, and he had no way to know which was in more danger.

"Any allies available?"

"None in the area. I could signal for assistance if you like."

He thought about it but decided he didn't want to over-react and potentially inspire action on the part of his adversaries. "Track all enemies. If you see them get closer or do more than follow, put the call out. Until then, let's handle it ourselves. Flying mode."

The display in his goggles adjusted to show the air currents that would take him up, take him down, or simply support him in level flight. He crossed to a different part of the roof in order to access the breeze he wanted and checked to be sure the grapnel launcher on his arm was ready to go in case of trouble. It was, naturally, exactly like all his gear. *Kayleigh and Deacon don't mess around.*

He leapt into space and pressed the button on his chest to toggle the flight functionality. The wide wings on the top and the shorter wings below them folded out of their container and caught the current, and in seconds, he soared in the general direction of his friends. His visual field displayed all the information he needed to keep track of, but Gwen made it easier by overlaying a course for him. She'd chosen to send him toward Professor Charlotte, and he agreed with the decision. Manny would be more on guard than ever and more likely to seek help or duck into a friendly shop for cover. The professor, however, would be as self-confident as she always was.

His respect for Charlotte Stanley was complete and he believed that in most situations, she would be able to take care of herself. The Remembrance scumbags, though, were a class of threat that the group of older folks who commemorated the Silver Griffins had probably never faced and perhaps never even conceived of. It was his job to ensure her confidence didn't actually result in her injury. He banked right and down, then caught another current that increased his speed toward the target. "Street view." The overlay map and dots vanished, replaced by a downward view of the people following his friend. From above, he couldn't make out much about them, other than what he thought was aggressive body language in the way they walked. "Not helpful. Other cameras?"

"None available in the area." It wasn't surprising. The well-to-do who populated the neighborhood she walked through didn't particularly like the idea of surveillance. On any other day, he would have been fine with that. Today, it was a solid irritant.

"How sure are we that these are enemies?"

"They met up with the people fleeing the burning house before they began to follow." She played the video of that meeting, again from a high angle, and he recognized the figures he'd battled inside.

"Okay. That's good enough for me. Find me a takedown location."

The AI was silent for almost half a minute before she gave him a map. There was a place where the professor would walk past the entrance to an alley, which would permit Rath to draw the fight into that space and away from most prying eyes. He was about to commit to the action when the situation changed. Two more red dots appeared beside his targets. "Gwen?"

"The enemies who were trailing Emanuel have joined the ones following Professor Charlotte."

"That'll make things more challenging. Call for help, just in case. We go in as planned."

As he leaned into the glide that would commit him to the fight to come, the thing he had been most concerned about occurred. The four pursuers grabbed Professor Charlotte and dragged her into the alley he'd intended to use to keep them away from her. Once the extra foes had appeared, his options had more or less vanished, but he had still held out hope for an outcome that ensured her escape. *Gotta play the hand you're dealt. Or cut it off and put a chainsaw on the stump.* He snorted at the terrible joke and angled himself for his final descent.

His original plan had been to employ a Batman-style move and snatch one of them in flight, pull them along, and drop them from a height. He'd never tried it, but Gwen's simulations suggested that with enough momentum, it might work. Now, however, he was at plan C—or maybe D—and still trying to settle the details. At the last minute, he decided to use one of the attackers to help him to stop.

He aimed his right arm ahead as he soared into the alley at high speed, about ten feet up, and pressed the button to collapse his wings with his left hand. He triggered the grapnel, and the spike rocketed forward to seek a target as the cable spun out behind it. Its flight ended when it stabbed deep into the upper arm of a man who brandished a pistol near Professor Charlotte, and Rath's velocity was cut to a fraction of his original speed when the line locked and yanked his anchor off his feet. The troll skidded to a stop and triggered the safety line's retraction, and the man screamed as the metal ripped out of his flesh. *One down if not out. Three left.*

Two of them turned to him with looks of anger on their faces, while the third lashed a punch at Professor Charlotte. The woman dodged, and the man's fist struck the brick wall behind her and left him howling in pain. She ducked out of the alley at a run, and the troll grinned.

"Surrender, morons. I am the law." The nearest responded by raising his wand and launching a wide cone of flame. Rath fired the grapnel upward toward the fire escape he'd noticed earlier and let the line carry him above the attack. While still in motion, he drew two blades and threw them both, one at each of his unharmed opponents. The wizard who wasn't trying to burn him to a crisp used his wand to block it, while the other failed to react in time. He screamed when the blade pierced him in the hand and he dropped his wand.

Rath leapt the dozen feet to the asphalt, rolled to absorb the impact, and found his feet beside the man who'd taken the grapnel to his arm and had now managed to rise to his knees. The troll lashed out with his batons to deliver a simultaneous strike to both of the man's temples, and he collapsed instantly. Gwen warned him of an impending attack from behind, and he flipped to the side to avoid the stream of icicles that almost found its target. He turned and ran forward, choosing an angle that would put the wizard with the knife between him and the remaining mage. As he neared him, he flinched toward the attacker but circled away at the last moment and engaged with the one with the broken fist. When he stabbed him with his shock batons, his adversary stiffened and fell senseless. The troll stopped and reversed course and his agility saved him from yet another magical assault, this time a cone of force that hammered into the brick wall and caused a flurry of shards in all directions.

Idiots. He turned to the unharmed wizard and smiled at him. "Take your best shot." Rath blurred into motion as the man cast, drew his final two blades, and hurled them at his foe. The flames washed over and around him but the anti-magic deflectors consumed the energy and shunted the power of the spell away from him. His knives struck true and drove powerfully into the man's shoulders, and he charged forward and delivered a jumping kick to the stunned mage's face. He went down hard with the troll on top of him. The last wizard, realizing he was alone, cradled his impaled hand and bolted toward the alley exit. Rath took a step toward him, ready to launch the grapnel and haul him back, but the mage suddenly stood tall, spun, and fell as blood spurted from his chest.

The troll stepped to the side and pressed his back to the wall. "Gwen, what happened?"

"Sniper." She slid a map into his display that displayed a blue dot where the bullet had come from. It was from far enough away that only an expert could have taken the shot.

It had to be Amadeo. He wasn't sure what the assassin wanted, what his endgame was, or why he had any interest in what Rath was up to but once again, he was in debt to him, both for the initial warning and for keeping an eye on him after. He shook his head. *That man is really good at what he does. I hope he stays on our side—or at least doesn't join the other side.*

He sighed and gave Gwen the orders to recall the other

ARES agents and summon ambulances and police. That done, he hurried off to find Professor Charlotte and escorted her away from the scene, congratulating her as she told him the story—several times—of how she managed to dodge the punch and get the best of the hoodlum.

CHAPTER SIXTEEN

Sloan slipped into the darkened Italian restaurant with no small amount of trepidation. The summons from Murray had been polite but couched in terms that left no doubt it was not an optional request. He was encouraged to see that the man sat alone at a table in the back, drinking a glass of white wine that stood out in contrast to the smart black suit he wore. *Another sartorial step up. Impressive.*

Mur rose to shake his hand and took his seat again. The undercover agent sat opposite him, and a server bustled up immediately to take their orders. Both men opted for pasta in a red sauce, Mur's a spicy Diavolo and his own a smoother Bolognese. A tall glass of Forst beer appeared a moment later, and he took a slow sip. They engaged in small talk before and during the meal, and Sloan's tension grew with each passing minute. Finally, after coffee had been served, the other man turned the conversation to business.

"So, Tommy, what do you think about me taking over for Marcus?"

He scratched the stubble on his face. "I think it's great. You were the boss's right-hand man so it makes total sense."

His companion gestured dismissively. "Cut the suck-up nonsense. What do you think?" The insistence behind the question signaled that perhaps he wasn't as confident as he liked to portray about the transition.

Sloan spread his hands to the sides and tried to appear thoughtful and non-threatening. "I think you'll be great at it. Everyone knows you and everyone trusts you. So, you totally can do it. The real question might be whether you want to do it." Mur sighed and indicated for him to continue. "Seriously, that witch is crazy, man. Certifiable. There's no telling what kind of scary stuff she'll drag us into. Maybe it's time..." He paused in order to seem conflicted, then shrugged. "Maybe it's time to go our own way, you know? Take the human side of the gang and set up our own thing away from the wackos."

The other man sighed again. "I can't deny that I've had some of the same thoughts. The problem is that we don't have adequate power to make it happen. We might be able to grow fast enough to hold our own against any other regular criminals in town, but if we try to break away, you know that evil witch will come to teach us a lesson about how inferior we are to them."

The agent nodded. It was almost undoubtedly an accurate representation of how the scene would play out. "So, is it official, or what?"

He shrugged. "We have a meeting at the base in an hour.

It's possible she'll confirm it. I guess it's equally possible that she might do any other damn thing as well, though." He shook his head. "This stuff used to be easy, you know? I've been in the game since I was a kid. But these magicals take it to a whole different level—one I'm not sure I really like playing on."

"I hear you, boss man, and I agree." He smiled to show he wasn't trying to cut Mur down. "But I guess those are the cards we're dealt right now. I suppose the other option is to fade and start up somewhere else."

Mur laughed, and there was a hopeless note to it. "This city has been my home since the day I was born. I know it here. I sense the currents and I can tell if trouble's coming simply by the way people walk down the street. I wouldn't have that in another town."

"But you might not have insane witches to deal with either."

"Do you think anywhere is safe from their kind anymore?" It was an offhand question and seemed to carry no weight, but he sensed a note of desire for such a place as well.

"No, I don't. I really don't. It's a brave new damned world in here, my friend."

He shook his head. "Damned might be a good word for it. Let's get to the meeting. Can I give you a lift?"

"Sure."

The atmosphere in the warehouse was charged with uncertainty. The different factions gathered in their own areas, as usual—the magicals clustered in one large group to the right of the entrance and the humans in separate huddles on the left. *It kind of represents the situation well. The magicals have it all together and we are divided and confused.* Sloan laughed inwardly. *Confusion to our enemies and all that, so I guess it's a good thing. It doesn't feel good from this position, though.* He followed a step behind Murray as the big man circulated among the humans, shook hands, and talked in a low voice. Occasionally, he darted a distrustful glance at the wizards and witches.

Sloan's talent gave him nothing from the magicals, but he sensed a great deal from the other side of the room. Fear, mainly, but also resentment. Surprisingly, more than one seemed to have bad feelings about their former leader, although that might have been emotionally mixed up with the current situation. He didn't get the full mind-reading impact of his magic, only the general sense, so he couldn't be sure. Wherever the truth of that might lie, it boded well for Murray stepping into the primary role as he looked to have the trust of most of the people on the left side of the room.

Everyone present turned as the crazy witch in charge made her typical entrance and slammed the office door after she stepped through it onto the metal staircase. Her boots rang with each step, and Sarah stopped halfway down, exactly as Vincente had been wont to do before her. The agent tuned out her opening words and focused instead on Murray's response. The man was rigid, clearly caught between his desire for authority and the fear they all had in one degree or another of the woman who'd vanished into a portal and returned changed, at best, and irreparably broken at worst. He returned to the moment when Murray and several men moved forward and the man in black gestured for him to join them.

Reluctantly, he trailed the other four up the stairs and his sense of foreboding grew with each step that brought them closer to the office. In all too short a time, they were inside the room and stood awkwardly while she sat behind the desk and put her feet on it. The idea of attacking her right then, of ending it all, flitted through his mind but he pushed it away. *Tommy Ketchum wouldn't have such thoughts. He's a good soldier if a little slow.* He forced a neutral look onto his face and waited.

The witch pointed at Mur. "Sit, Murray." He complied, and she stared at him for a few seconds in silence before she nodded. "The humans need someone to follow. I see no reason why it can't be you. Even though you were close to our dearly departed half-man Marcus, I won't hold that against you." Her tone was gleeful when she referred to the demise of their former leader. "Will you pledge your loyalty to me and to this organization?"

Mur straightened and nodded. "I will."

She clapped and thumped her feet on the floor as she sat up. "Excellent. So. Now that we have a chain of command in place, I have a task for you and your people." She gestured with her wand and an aerial view of the city appeared and hovered over the desk. The perspective zoomed from the center to a building on the outskirts, which was highlighted with a yellow tint. "This place is of great interest. We discovered its presence when we raided the police station. They didn't know that we also had a magical who is good with electronics, and she accessed their computer records. It turns out there is a holding facility here in our city where evidence is kept awaiting state and federal trials. Items of power that rightfully belong to us are doubtless in that building ."

Bloody hell. Another one? He'd managed to avoid taking part in the action at the police station by faking drunkenness. It hadn't earned him any points and in fact, Murray had sat him down and given him a talking to about it, but it had kept him out of his teammates' way. He was sure he wouldn't be able to pull the same trick again without being discovered and killed.

Mur nodded. "Timetable?"

She gestured airily. "At your discretion, but within a week."

"Will you give us magical support?"

Sarah scowled. "After the failure of the last attempt to steal artifacts, I believe the witches and wizards need additional training before they venture out again." It was the closest she'd ever come to criticizing the magicals who worked for her, and he wondered if it was merely an excuse to send the humans out alone. "So no, it will only be your people." She leaned forward and pointed a finger at their new leader. "And there's one other thing, and this is paramount. We must keep the details of the operation strictly between those of us in this room. Somewhere, there is a leak in the organization. I have looked carefully at each one of you and cleared you of suspicion. Do not share anything until the last minute, and even then, only share that an operation exists, never what or where it is." She settled into her chair again. "This must go well, and we must keep it a secret."

Sloan's moment of panic at the mention of a leak had passed by the time she finished speaking and dismissed them. He walked down the stairs and out of the warehouse in a haze, and his mind was still spinning when Mur dropped him off at his car. When the large man had driven away, he cruised slowly through the city with one hand on the wheel and scant focus on the road. Between hasty glances to make sure his driving remained acceptable, he composed a message on a hidden chat app to Kayleigh to alert her to the upcoming raid. It sent and was electronically shredded into nothingness. He kept the app open all the way home and glanced at it every ten seconds to see if there was a reply, knowing there likely wouldn't be one anytime soon.

He was surprised when it arrived as he parked outside his apartment. It was short, simple, and unsatisfying. *Do Nothing. D.*

So, a message directly from the boss giving me no useful information whatsoever. He sighed, unlocked the front door, and looked around at the shabby furniture. *I swear to heaven I will get an undercover gig as a posh playboy one of these days or die trying.*

CHAPTER SEVENTEEN

K ayleigh smacked her palms on the worktable in agitation, and her boss raised an eyebrow at her. "Really, don't hold back."

The tech reclined in her chair and folded her arms. "He has to come out. Now. The danger is ridiculous, and we made it worse by trying to bug the place." The guilt the other woman felt was clearly a driving factor in her zeal to get Sloan out of his assignment with the Remembrance. *The fact that she's personally involved doesn't really change the validity of her argument, though. And to imagine that we're all not personally involved is probably naïve, too.*

She sighed. "There are bigger issues at hand, and you know it. These bastards are planning something big, and he may be our only way to discover what's going on."

Deacon stepped into the lab and joined them, standing at the edge of the table she and Kayleigh were seated at to create a triangle rather than an oppositional team. His voice was soft and understanding. "We have several competing priorities here and no clear means to choose between them because the stakes are so high. Arguing about it won't help." He tapped the table corner to activate its display function and used a finger to write on it. "Our first concern is Sloan's safety. The second concern is intelligence on the group. How about we start with that?"

Diana nodded, impressed at the way he'd defused the situation. *Kayleigh was right, he was a good addition.* The blonde tech spoke in a slightly less aggressive tone. "I get that we need to know what they're up to as long as they're still relevant. But why don't we simply go in, destroy them, and render them irrelevant?"

She shrugged. "It's the classic espionage problem. They've been able to pull in new members seemingly at will, which suggests they have a network in operation. If we cut off the head—the only visible part—the body still remains. The only option is to continue to thin them out until they have to throw all their resources into the fight. Then, we can eliminate them."

The blonde tech growled, "There's no way to be sure that's true."

Her lab partner placed a hand on her arm, and her shoulders sagged a little.

"There's no way to be sure it's not true, and the penalty for being wrong is severe," Diana replied, sighed, and shook her head. "We need to pull Cara and Tony in for this discussion. She's being hunted like I am, and losing our insider could have consequences for her. And Tony is probably the only one of us who's worked most often with undercover agents. Friday, are Cara and Tony around?"

Her AI spoke through the room's speakers. "They both have status set to available. Neither is currently on site."

She nodded. "Have them meet us soonest at Stan's." She turned to the others. "Let's go hash this out once and for all."

Diana and Bryant had discovered the hole-in-the-wall tavern during one of his visits to the city. The front section held a long bar with Pittsburgh-related paraphernalia decorating the wall behind it. The back room contained wobbly tables and chairs with ripped vinyl. Despite the shabbiness, the barbecue was to die for and during normal meal hours, there was no way to get a table. This late in the evening and after the early, main, and late dinner crowds had come and gone, the establishment claimed not to serve food but still did as long as there was some left and only to customers who knew about it.

The owner was behind the bar and recognized her as she walked in. "Diana, it's been a while. What's shakin'?" Several of the universally male and predominantly western-styled patrons turned to look at her, but she didn't recognize any of them.

"Nada, Stan man. Came in for a bite and some privacy. There will be five of us."

He grinned and nodded. "The back's all yours. Go ahead and put the rope up."

She led the way to the rear and obediently hooked the piece of rope that sealed the back section with a "closed" sign hanging from it. The others pushed two tables together and Duncan shoved a wad of folded napkins under one of the feet to keep it from wobbling. They sat and a bucket of beer bottles appeared. It was a sign of how fantastic the food was that Diana was willing to frequent a place that didn't believe in draft beer. Stan had explained that the costs were too high because his drinking crowd was irregular and tended toward whiskey. She'd shaken her head in despair, but when he provided them with an assortment of craft bottles, her mood had improved. Today's selection was equally as good, and she snatched the nearest IPA, popped the top with the opener attached to the bucket, and took a sip.

The others did the same, and they talked about the situation with the oversight committee while they waited. The techs continued to run surveillance, and while the amount of information had diminished somewhat, it hadn't stopped altogether. They both thought there was still something worth digging for, so they continued to do so. Cara and Tony arrived within a minute of each other. The second in command tossed her helmet onto a nearby table and the investigator wore a bowling shirt with a team name on it.

Kayleigh looked at him. "Really? You're like a walking stereotype."

The former detective laughed. "Sure, woman who stays up all night video gaming with twelve-year-olds. I'm the stereotype."

Deacon laughed and she hit him, which drew a burst of laughter from the others. Diana sobered quickly, though. "Choose a drink, you two. You'll need it. We'll talk first, then feast. Stan is holding stuff in the warmer for us."

They obliged, and the owner proved his customer senses were firing perfectly by bringing bowls of chips, pretzels, and pickles to the table with another bucket of bottles. She nodded at Deacon. "Lay it out for us again."

He straightened and set his bottle down. "We've come to a moment of crisis with Sloan. There's suspicion of a traitor within the gang. We have two primary concerns—his safety and the need to be informed of what the enemy group is up to. Kayleigh has already suggested eliminating them, but the boss has rejected that."

"Because we're not sure we have all of them," Cara interrupted.

Deacon nodded. "So, that leaves us with those questions, which seem to be impossible to reconcile."

No one spoke for a minute, so Diana said, "Let's brainstorm it. All ideas are welcome."

"Pull him out and damn the consequences," Kayleigh said. "We can deal with stuff as it comes."

"Pull him out but bug the place again," Tony countered,

Cara shook her head but kept to the rules and didn't criticize any of the suggestions that had gone before. "Keep him on the string a little longer but create an escape plan."

Deacon shrugged. "I think the best course of action is to protect our own. Maybe we could set a trap for them or something?"

There were a few more potential plans shared, but they were all variations on the same themes. Nothing was compelling enough to make the decision easy. Diana was about ready to opt for the status quo when Tony belched politely and spoke as he stretched for another beer. "I have a question, though. How did our boy find out about the upcoming op?"

She had traded messages with him for the details before

they'd come to the tavern. "The witch called him, the new human leader, and three others up to the office."

"Why?"

She tilted her head at him in confusion. "Why what?"

"Why did she do it that way rather than telling everyone at once?"

Deacon shrugged. "Maybe she didn't want the magical side knowing they were being cut out?"

Cara tapped a finger against a tooth. "Yeah, that could be. But what if it wasn't that? What if there was a reason those particular people were in the room?"

Diana realized what they were referring to. "Do you think they might specifically suspect one of those five? Or that they're choosing people at random to search for leaks?"

Tony nodded. "It's what we would do in a similar situation—feed information to a small group as a test. If it doesn't leak, move on to the next. If it does, you can drill down further."

Kayleigh sounded more worried than she had earlier. "Or simply kill them all out of hand. This means we need to let the warehouse thing happen. We can't afford to out him."

Diana rapped her knuckles on the table. "We can't. That is not an option. If it's what they describe, it's too valuable to allow the contents to be stolen. We'll check it, of course, but I've heard of it before and all indications are that there's inventory inside our evil friends would love to get their hands on. Dammit, we should have identified this when they targeted the police station—it's the logical next step for them." She drummed her fingers on the table and thought hard while her people remained silent. Finally, she sighed. "Kayleigh's correct. We've run Sloan as long as we can. I say we pull him out. But"—she turned to Cara—"you have to be on board with this since you have a price on your head."

Her second in command nodded decisively. "I believe it's the right moment for him to come in out of the cold. Let's make it happen. But let's do it in a way that will hurt those scumbags the most."

There were smiles on everyone's face, and Diana realized she had one on hers, as well. "Okay, then. We're decided. Deacon, tell Stan to bring us the food. Now that we know our objective, we can eat and plan at the same time. Before we leave, we need to have a solid idea of how to both crush their raid on the warehouse and get Face out safely."

CHAPTER EIGHTEEN

Murray hadn't wasted any time, which was why Sloan was now in a panel van with a group of the other humans from the Remembrance gang and on the way to the warehouse. *Honestly, his assumption of power and inspiration to move are fairly impressive.* He felt disconnected from reality by the suddenness of the action. A standby notice from Diana had arrived the night before but he'd received no communication since. His signal to let the team know they were on the move had been released into cyberspace when he'd climbed in the vehicle fifteen minutes earlier. The rest of the squad looked as confused as he felt so apparently, Mur had sprung the op on all of them.

The six with him were bouncy, excited, and eager to plunder the location and prove their worth to the new boss. He wasn't any of those things, and the waves of enthusiasm that constantly washed over him were irritating beyond words. *Idiots.* The driver and their leader beside him probably felt the same. They had only brought eight people, as Sarah had assured them the facility would be mostly unguarded once they cleared the main checkpoint. Two or three men on patrol at the most, she'd said. Sloan didn't believe it would be that easy because nothing ever was, but it had certainly opened the opportunity to run the operation on short notice.

Mur spoke over the headphones they all wore for the job. "Okay, listen. We'll stop about a quarter-mile out. Tommy and Randall will eliminate the guard at the gate from behind while we drive up. Then, you'll let us in and the van will pull up to the loading dock. We'll split into two teams to look for patrols and gear. Randall mans the entrance in the guard's shirt or jacket and hat, and Murph stays with the truck. It should be an easy one. We can be in and out in ten minutes—thirty at most if things aren't clearly labeled." He had confided to the agent that they had the item numbers for the crates holding the items they had been sent to retrieve, thanks to the electronic incursion into the police computer system.

He shook his head. *The last thing crazy Sarah needs is more magical artifacts.* He glanced at his phone one final time before he put it away and saw the message from Kayleigh's assumed identity.

Urgent that we reach you regarding the senate race in your state! Please reply as soon as possible on our new website. He concentrated to suppress the adrenaline that blazed through him as he read those words.

Finally. And what absolutely useless timing. The word "urgent" told him that he was to break from his cover and vanish at the earliest opportunity. The reference to the new website meant he was to use the option they'd sent him the night before, which involved a different safe house than originally planned—assuming he could get to it. Their first choice, long before, had been near the warehouse. Now, apparently, they wanted him to have more distance from their enemies. *That suits me fine.*

He looked around the truck with fresh eyes. There were five of them, plus himself, the driver, and Mur. He couldn't think of any means to derail the mission, given how outnumbered he was, and if the situation devolved into a shootout, he might cause the death of innocent people, not to mention put himself in the line of fire from both sides. Plus, he didn't want them to have the artifacts, and it was always possible he could find a way to prevent it. Maybe luck would be with him and the guards would catch some of the others and improve the numbers.

No, I'll have to ride this out and try to escape after. He resisted the urge to verify that his pistol was in his pocket and wished he hadn't insisted that Tommy Ketchum was a handgun-only kind of criminal.

The van stopped and Randall led the way out the back. Sloan followed, closed the door quietly behind him, and trailed the other man into the bushes beside the road. The federal evidence facility was at the end of a long dirt track bounded on both sides by grass and shrubs. Its security relied on the high metal fence topped with razor wire around the perimeter, on the guards who patrolled inside, and on the checkpoint he and Randall currently headed toward. Sloan considered shooting him to put the base on intrusion alert, but that risked him being immediately pursued by both groups without ensuring the artifacts would stay safe. He shook his head. *Wait. The time will come.*

He moved in a crouch behind his partner and they approached the guard, who had stepped out of his shack to talk to the driver. Randall raised his weapon and Sloan pushed it down, placed a finger to his lips, and took the lead. He crept up unseen, put the sentry in a headlock, and squeezed down sufficiently to cut off the blood flow but not enough to kill him. Randall helped control the man's struggles by wrapping him in a bear hug and together, they wrestled his unconscious form into the guard post. Sloan triggered the button to raise the barrier so the van could go through, then returned it to its former position and ran to jump through the now open rear doors. Behind them, Randall stepped into his role of impersonating the gate guard, wearing the man's shirt and hat.

Well, at least that's one innocent who might survive this debacle. I hope his friends return the favor if we run into them. The van continued to the building and made a two-point turn to back against the loading dock. The team emerged soundlessly, and Sloan stepped beside Mur. The big man pointed at the team member closest. "You're with us. The rest of you go counter-clockwise. We'll go clockwise. Find any guards, take them out silently, and look for the boxes. You have the numbers, right?" Everyone nodded. Sloan didn't have them, but he decided the assumption all along had been that he would accompany Mur.

Randall spoke through a crackle and hiss over their headphones. "Incoming. I let them through the gate. It's a delivery."

Murray gestured quickly and the three of them ducked behind a pile of nearby boxes. Hopefully, on the far side of the building, the other team had done the same. Sloan peered around to see what was going on. The new arrivals entered through a side door carrying crates of evidence, accompanied by loud laughter, crashing, and banging. One of the guards on duty arrived to direct them, and the agent kept his head down and prayed for things not to go wrong. *It would be exactly like a classic cop movie if I was killed in this damn warehouse after I'd already received the signal to get out.* He breathed a sigh of relief when the guard checked the . paperwork with the delivery driver and turned to hold the door open for them to leave.

At that moment, one of the idiots in the other team lost his cool and the first indication of trouble came when a rifle spat bullets in a staccato series. The barrage stitched through the guard and peppered the side of the building to leave scattered holes. Mur, Sloan, and their partner looked at one another for a shocked moment before they darted out from behind their boxes toward the action. Another two guards had joined the fight and now fired at the other squad from a distance, while the two who had made the delivery found their own cover to assist the defenders. It was a momentary standoff and Sloan muttered to Murray, "We're on the clock now. Someone's sure to have called it in." He hoped the other man would decide to abandon the operation—hoped it with all that he was worth—but naturally, he chose the opposite approach.

"Then we need to kill these bastards quickly and get our job done. You two go right, I'll go left." The agent took the lead and tried his utmost to slow their progress while he looked for a way to turn the situation, but nothing presented itself. By the time they reached the far side, two of their men were bleeding out on the floor and all the defenders had fallen, some wounded and the others dead. Murray paced furiously for a minute and vented his anger in a series of yells. One of the guards' radios crackled with the news that backup was on the way.

The big man turned to the team, his demeanor suddenly calm and businesslike. "Randall, come on in and ride shotgun in the van. Sloan and I will search over there." He indicated the left part of the building. "You two take the other side. We have seven minutes, then we're out of here. Find something worth stealing so this whole effort isn't wasted."

CHAPTER NINETEEN

They circled the stacks while Mur called codes out as they advanced and Sloan checked the boxes. When the first few numbers of the sequence matched, they'd stop and check the rest but progress was slow. The crates were arranged like the blocks of a city, with a grid of passages spaced between them. They rested on shelves that reached six feet high—which seemed stupid in the multi-story warehouse—but it fit with the overall sense that the building was an impermanent installation, some kind of overflow facility or temporary storage rather than a final destination.

The other group shouted that they'd discovered something, and while Mur's mood lightened noticeably, he pushed them forward as fast as he could go. They were near the back of the space when Randall announced, "Two minutes left. We need to get the hell out of here." The others reported that they would return to the van in the same moment that Mur noticed a crate that matched his numbers. He turned with an excited look and said,

"Tommy, help me pull this down." Sloan complied, not knowing what else he could do, and they set the heavy wooden box on the floor.

He looked over his shoulder. "Mur, we should really start moving toward the exit. You heard him."

The man in black shook his head as he removed a small crowbar from his belt. "Randall's a worrier. If he says two minutes, it's actually at least four and probably six. That's why I left him at the guard post." He wedged the lever under one side and pushed it down, then repeated the process as he circled the crate until the lid was no longer attached. He shoved it open, and both men peered inside.

A thick grey foam sheet contained cutouts where objects had lain. Sloan had no idea what artifacts looked like, but from the way his partner paled, he guessed the other man did. He stared with bewilderment on his face. "What the hell?"

The agent shrugged. "Wrong box?" he suggested weakly.

Mur shook his head before suddenly, he raised it. "The witch was right. We do have a leak. They found out about this before we got here and took the good stuff out. But how? It was only the six of us who knew about it." His voice trailed off and Sloan jumped in quickly.

"Maybe the base is bugged again—you know, like last time?"

The leader shook his head and took a step away. "It's checked daily. There's no way they could have overheard our conversation in the office. No, it couldn't be Sarah, and it's not you or me, so it must be one of the others." He shoved the crowbar back in his belt and drew his gun. "And

I'll make sure the traitor pays before we leave this warehouse."

He was on the verge of trying to talk him out of it when his talent activated unexpectedly. The words inside Mur's head seemed to voice themselves in his mind as if the man had spoken out loud. *I don't know why you did it and I don't know how you could have done it. This is the greatest betrayal of all. I thought we were friends, Tommy.* The warning gave him an instant's notice, barely enough time to act as the pistol swept toward his face. He lunged, rammed his body into the other man's, and drove forward with all his strength. One palm covered his attacker's mouth, and he slammed a punch into Mur's wrist to deaden the nerves of the hand holding the gun. The blow jolted the weapon aside as the man's finger squeezed on the trigger and the sharp report set Sloan's ears ringing. *Shit.*

He landed on top of the bigger man and delivered a nasty head butt to his face, stunning him. A quick kick dislodged the gun, but as he turned to knock Mur out, his assailant's fist connected with his temple and he tumbled to the side. He forced himself quickly to his feet to find his opponent had done the same and now gripped the crowbar in his still-functioning hand, his knuckles white around the metal. Mur yelled, "Ketch is the traitor. Help me kill him."

"Damn it, Murray, it did not have to go down like this." He said the words as he attacked again, ducked under the wild swing with the crowbar, and delivered a one-two punch to his opponent's solar plexus and his jaw. The man collapsed again, and Sloan drew his pistol and aimed it at him.

Mur glared at him and rage and betrayal warred for supremacy in his expression. "How could you, Tommy? What did they offer you?"

He shook his head. "It's not your fault. This is what I do." He held the weapon trained squarely on the downed man and his finger tightened.

I can't do it. He released the trigger with a sigh. "Stay down. Don't follow me, or I'll have to kill you. Tell the others the same. If anyone follows, they die." He broke into a run toward the back of the building as gunshots rang out from the middle of the warehouse. One raised the hair on his neck as it passed a little too close for comfort and he heard the ricochet of another as he cut hastily into a side lane.

Mur bellowed, "Let him go. We need to get out of here," but he had no way of knowing if the others would obey. He slammed the door as he exited, heard the sirens nearby, and focused solely on not getting swept up with the others who would definitely kill him before they reached the safety of a police station.

Sloan sprinted toward the front of the facility, keenly aware that the only way he could escape the fence was through the sentry gate. He slid into cover when he reached it and waited for the cars to pass. They were converging on the warehouse, and as he had no idea of the status of the men he'd entered with, he had to stay hidden from both sides. He scampered through when the moment presented itself and broke into a run to angle away from the building, remaining half-crouched and low in the grass so no one would see him.

After a mile, he judged he was safe from anything other

than a K-9 unit, and he hadn't seen or heard one. *Hopefully, the authorities are still busy with the Remembrance folks.* He sank to the ground, bone-tired but strangely happy. Sometimes, his undercover gigs ended with sadness and loss and he knew without a doubt he'd miss the Mur he'd befriended, if not the Mur who'd tried to kill him. But leaving this assignment would be a pleasure. He sent the message indicating he was clear, including the code words that verified he wasn't under duress, and waited for the cavalry to come and pick him up. Finally, after such a long time, he could go home.

CHAPTER TWENTY

For what felt like the first time in forever, the entire ARES team was together again. Bryant had even portaled in from DC for the occasion. Diana sat at the head of the rectangular table with her boyfriend at her left and Sloan at her right. Kayleigh claimed the chair next to the undercover agent and looked equal parts giddy and relieved that he was finally out. *It's good that she can set down whatever guilt she's carried over this since it wasn't deserved in the first place.*

They'd taken over the back room of a downtown restaurant for the evening, one Diana ate at often enough to know the owner reasonably well. The woman had been more than willing to let them use the space and to keep nosy people out of their affairs while they were there. The remainder of the team was seated around the table, passing plates of Middle Eastern food and teasing and joking with each other.

She turned to Sloan and spoke quietly so her voice

wouldn't carry beyond him. "So, let's take care of business first. What do we need to know about the witch?"

He rolled his neck and took a moment to collect his thoughts. After almost an entire day asleep, he seemed in much better shape than when they'd picked him up the night before. He'd shaved the remnants of his character off —aside from the longer hairstyle, which actually looked good on him. There was an ease about him she hadn't seen since the team's Face had gone undercover. "First, she's crazy. And I don't mean that in the typical sense of the word. The woman is literally, certifiably, insane. I can't say whether she was before she was banished to that other world or whatever, but she came back broken. Since then, the damage has only gotten worse. With her in charge, there's no real way to guess what they'll do."

She nodded and Bryant asked, "Do you think we could end the threat if we eliminated her?"

Sloan considered the question for a moment before he shook his head decisively. "She wants everyone to believe she's the highest authority, but I don't buy it."

Kayleigh invited herself into the conversation. "She's not. We've heard her taking orders from someone. Maybe you should listen to the tapes and see if you can get anything extra out of them that we haven't."

There was a surge of laughter from the far end of the table, and Tony wore the pleased look that signaled successful delivery of one of the punch lines he always had near to hand. She smiled at him, and he returned it before he turned to the people around him to start another of his exaggerated stories. She faced Sloan again. "So, other than Sarah, what's essential for us to be aware of?"

The team's Face took a sip of his champagne—Cara had insisted that celebrations required champagne, and who was she to argue?—and leaned back with a sigh. "The human leader, Murray, is a good guy, for a criminal. He wants to do as little harm as possible, I think." She saw from the way his face twisted that saying the next part was hard for him. "It may be something we can exploit. I don't know if he'll be able to bring himself to turn on the group, but if things go south, he might be willing to surrender rather than fight to the death." She nodded, encouraging him to continue. "The other humans in the gang are standard petty criminals. We have nothing to fear there except their numbers and a seemingly endless supply of replacements."

Kayleigh interrupted, "Do you know where they come from?"

"No. I honestly have no idea. Marcus and Murray kept that to themselves. I can say they never seemed concerned about it at all." The tech shot Diana a frustrated look and clearly had hoped for confirmation—or, more likely, refutation—of their concern about independent cells operating in the city. Sloan continued without noticing the silent exchange. "The magicals, on the other hand, seem a little harder to come by. I think that's why Sarah sent the humans out on their own for the last op. She's worried about losing her power base. Although, with Mur as their leader, it's not like there's a threat from them the way there was before." He shook his head. "I don't know. The games going on are all very mysterious."

"To some degree, that's because we've managed to eliminate a couple of their leaders so far," Bryant suggested.

"Losing top people is bound to throw any organization into chaos."

Diana slapped him on the arm. "Yeah, so you boss types need to take care of yourselves."

"I'm not the one with a prize on their head."

Sloan's voice was incredulous. "What?"

She sighed. "It appears our crazy witch enemy has put hits out on Cara and I. Bounty hunters have already made an attempt on her and managed to kill her motorcycle."

"Ouch. She loves that bike."

Kayleigh rolled her eyes. "Yes, the inanimate object is the important part of the story. Never mind the whole almost dying thing."

He laughed. "I'm merely saying I wouldn't want to be the person who shot it when she catches up to them, that's all."

They all joined him in laughter and when it subsided, Diana lowered her voice again. "What do you know about their artifacts? Why have they focused on gathering them?"

The agent shook his head. "The highest-level information is all kept from us, so I can't be sure. But Murray mentioned something about preparing for a big event and the need to gather resources beforehand. I can only assume that's what they plan to use them for."

Bryant drummed his fingers on the table. "If they're seeking and finding artifacts to empower all the subordinate magicals, it could make them extraordinarily dangerous."

"That's been their MO since the beginning, really, so it's unlikely they'd change now," Diana added. "But it is concerning. Sloan, did you hear them mention the kemana?"

He shook his head. "I think they're done down there, for now at least. Sarah hasn't mentioned it, anyway, and Mur didn't say anything about it, either."

"Well, that's something."

"How close are they to pulling off whatever the big thing is?" Kayleigh asked.

Sloan shrugged. "I'd say more than days but less than months. No one seems really sure and they seem to be in a holding pattern. But we definitely need to move with our preparations, regardless."

The tech sighed and looked away like she didn't want anyone to see her reaction. Diana put her head in her hand, the champagne warmth transforming into a headache. "So, what would you recommend we do? We've all discussed strategies to deal with the Remembrance until we're tired of looking at one another, but you haven't been around. What's your read on the situation?"

He straightened and looked thoughtful. "I think we need to continue surveillance, that's a given. If we can identify and disrupt more of their small operations, that would be a win. It might be worth dropping a new round of bugs into the warehouse simply to unsettle them. Basically, anything that increases the emotional pressure on Sarah will make her less logical and more unpredictable. Maybe it's possible to pressure her into a mistake or something." He shook his head. "All of that is dangerous, though, because she's so volatile. There's no way to know how she'll turn at any given moment. We have to be prepared for anything."

Diana called to Hank across the room and he came over immediately. She looked up at his towering form. "Is the mobile armory ready?"

He grinned. "One hundred percent, boss, as soon as we have Sloan's preferred kit on board."

"Pack extras. We might find ourselves in a run and gun situation with these Remembrance bastards. If we do take them on, we need to make sure it's a clean sweep." She looked at Bryant, and he nodded. *Plus, if it becomes necessary to invoke Project Adonis, the truck might be our primary HQ for a while.* "Get backups of the AIs and any other vital computer equipment and devices on board, too." The large man frowned for an instant but gave her a nod and headed to the other side of the table, tapped Deacon on the shoulder, and drew him aside for a private conversation.

She looked at Kayleigh. "Be ready to go mobile as well. Just in case. We're not the most secret organization these days, and if they somehow get in here, we need to be able to continue to function." The tech nodded.

Sloan frowned. "I take it you've seen things that make you think something big is on the way, too?"

Diana chuckled in frustration. "Oh yes. So very many things. If there's a single thing that's clear, it's that a showdown is coming. One we can't afford to lose or our city will be in deep trouble."

"All our cities, "Bryant added. "You have to remember this is merely the tip of the iceberg."

She sighed. "True. All our cities." She stood and raised her voice. "Everyone, drink up and enjoy an extra dessert tonight. Tomorrow, the hard work begins and there's no end in sight. We have cities to protect and an incredibly annoying enemy organization we intend to smash into smithereens. Everyone will need to bring their best selves to the fight." *And that means I have to discover what the hell is up with Fury, and fast.*

She tapped Bryant on the shoulder. "Hey, G-Man, do you fancy a drink at the hotel across the street?"

He raised an eyebrow. "Only if it's room service."

She grinned and echoed his comment from the last time they'd been together. "I wouldn't have it any other way."

CHAPTER TWENTY-ONE

L echnas stared into the flames as he mused on the challenges his subordinates faced on Earth. It had seemed a simple plan to bring the kemanas into line and he had accomplished a few early successes. But first Dreven, and now Iressa, found their efforts thwarted by the human authorities. Plus, the information source he'd had on the inside of their organization had suddenly ceased communication, which suggested that those same authorities had eliminated the leak. He shook his head. *It is frustrating, to be sure. I see no clear opportunities to be had from these challenges so I'll need to identify new ones.* Fortunately, the flow of news from Earth's other forces continued unabated.

He stood and set his goblet of brandy on the table and walked deeper into the castle. The sparseness of his refuge soothed him, everything perfectly orderly and each item exactly where it was meant to be. Those he hired to clean were under strict orders not to change a thing—ever. He'd explained his wishes to each of them personally so they'd know the gravity of the situation, and he was confident the fear he'd instilled would achieve the desired result. And now, it was time to talk to other subordinates and possibly use that same fear to encourage their actions as well.

When he reached his dressing room, he carefully removed the comfortable velvet smoking jacket he wore when alone at home and hung it as he always did. He donned his armor—an impressive array of black leather and chainmail—and belted his swords on. The likelihood of him using them rather than his magic was minimal, but they added an implicit threat to all his dealings that gave him a subtle advantage. He carried three wands, a primary and two backups. The main one was in his sleeve, accessible with a practiced flick of the wrist. The others were cleverly hidden and would probably pass inspection if he were to be searched. *As if such a thing could ever happen. I would die fighting before I allowed myself to be captured.*

The corners of his mouth tilted into a scowl as he considered the situation again. It came down to the enemy leadership, as it always did. The body was nothing without a head, and in the case of Earth's authorities, they had identified two. *Diana Sheen and Cara Binot.* A less intelligent person might underestimate the danger posed by the two because they were women, but Lechnas had never been one to judge by such characteristics. Actions were what counted, and they had foiled a substantial number of operations attempted by his people. It was past time for them to be permanently removed from the board.

At his orders, Dreven had tagged each of the members of the circle with a magical tracer of his own invention. It had enabled him to keep track of their locations and was what had permitted him to leave the invitation for Iressa to visit. With the others, however, he was less inclined to allow them into his home. They hadn't yet shown enough value for such an honor. Instead, he'd arranged for the two of them to receive invitations to gather at a neutral location, where they should be arriving at any moment. He opened a portal to a hidden clearing in the forest, stepped through, and summoned another that would connect him to the small room at the rear of the tavern where they should be waiting. *There is no sense in letting anyone identify a potential path to my domain, after all.* He entered his destination and nodded at the two beings seated near the roaring fireplace. They were already eating and drinking, indicating that his orders to the owners of the establishment had been followed, which earned the serving girl a nod as well.

He sat between them, his chair a little more removed from the fire than theirs. He was far enough back that they each had to twist to look at him, a petty insult that he nonetheless enjoyed.

The Kilomea, Pesharn, was the first to speak. "Who are you and why did you call us here?"

Jarkko the dwarf added, "Not that we don't appreciate a free meal now and again, of course."

Lechnas nodded. "You do not know me, but I know of you both quite well. I am Lechnas, and until his recent demise, Dreven worked for me." To their credit, neither revealed the surprise they likely felt. Even if they'd known the recently dead wizard wasn't the top person in the chain, it was extremely unlikely they would have made the connection before he did it for them. "While the circle itself is no more, its work must continue. Thus my request for you to join me. It is time for all of us to take a more direct role in the happenings on Earth."

Pesharn shook her head. "I will not be a pawn again. Your underling had no comprehension of how to properly utilize my skills—or anyone else's."

The dwarf nodded and pointed at the Kilomea. "What she said. You'll have to make this well worth our while in order to convince either of us to help you. Your man was pathetic and selecting him does not reflect positively on your competence."

The wizard shrugged. "One does the best with what one has. For a time, Dreven was useful. Unfortunately, he proved too emotional and was compromised by the evolving situation. It was impossible to predict. It's impossible to know the strength of a new blade until it is quenched and tempered."

The two before him exchanged a glance and an unspoken communication appeared to pass between them. They turned to him, and the dwarf asked, "What did you have in mind?"

He smiled. "It's a task I believe you will enjoy immensely. It involves killing the people who have derailed your plans again and again."

The Kilomea showed her teeth in a wide grin. "Tell us more."

"Our enemies have acquired the pieces of Rhazdon's Vengeance, despite our efforts to retrieve them first. The second in command has the daggers, and the leader has recently retrieved the sword. The longer they possess the items, the more powerful they will become. We must strike now—and strike hard—to eliminate this threat." He nodded at them. "You two are the most skilled and the most bloodthirsty of the circle."

They looked at one another and laughed. Jarkko drawled, "Surely you have us mistaken with Iressa." All three of them chuckled at that, and Lechnas shook his head.

"Iressa has her own tasks but, like you, has accepted the invitation to work with me. Not as pawns, as you've said, but as partners. Although, make no mistake, I am in charge." They nodded, apparently content with the arrangement, and he continued. "We've created a distraction for these women by putting a bounty on them and offered money to Earth's criminal element to kill them. However, no one—except perhaps the figurehead witch we use in their city—actually believes this will succeed. Instead, it's simply an effort to soften them up and prepare the ground for the real experts."

Again, they nodded but did not speak. He asked, "Are you willing, then, to undertake the killing of these women? You can work together on both or each choose one, it matters not to me. The only thing that does matter is that, within the week, at least one of them is dead and the other follows soon after. Plans are coming to a head in the city, and they must not be allowed to interfere."

Pesharn folded her arms. "And our reward for accomplishing this for you?"

He grinned. "Name your price."

She paused and considered her response carefully. "The daggers." Her companion scowled and the wizard laughed inside.

"Done." *That was indeed a clever move, choosing the artifact that would be more appropriate for Jarkko, given his size. A dwarf with daggers is much more of a threat than one trying to wield an improperly sized sword. Although, if the rumors about the blade are true, she might discover her plan has backfired.*

"Then the sword for me," the dwarf grumbled. "I take it that means I will kill the leader?"

Lechnas held his hands out to his sides. "That would seem logical unless you wish to trust one another to deliver the artifacts you've chosen." They both shook their heads simultaneously and he nodded. "Well, then. Jarkko, Diana Sheen is your target. Pesharn, you will eliminate Cara Binot." He rose and stared at each of them in turn. "In the past, when members of the circle failed Dreven, punishment was lacking. Do not make the error of believing that I am as lenient. Return in victory or do not come back at all. Remember, no more than one week for the first and the other soon after."

He strode to the edge of the room, cast a portal, and stepped through it.

The wizard was in his chair by the fire again when Iressa joined him that evening. She was resplendent, as always, in her tight black dress, and the broach he'd given her was fastened at her shoulder. He remarked upon it, and she smiled. *Ah, the game. If I had any interest in romance, you would be tempting, witch. However, my only desire is power. There will be time for all the rest after.* He gestured for her to sit and she took her seat with demure elegance. "Thank you for coming to visit me once again."

"Thank you for inviting me."

He nodded. "Matters come to a head. I have set your former colleagues from the circle new tasks. They will eliminate the leadership of the human authorities above Stonesreach."

She shook her head dubiously. "That promise has been made more than once, I'm afraid. They have proven stronger than any sent against them."

"That's why this time, Jarkko and Pesharn will do the deed themselves."

She raised an eyebrow. "Really? How did you persuade them to do that? And why did you choose them after their former failures?"

Lechnas smiled. "Who among us has not failed?" He saw her flinch as the reference to her own near-death at the hands of the humans hit home. "I have offered them two things. First—and perhaps most importantly—the chance at redemption, in their eyes and in mine. But also, the material reward of the daggers and the sword."

Iressa frowned. "If those were on offer, I should have been given the opportunity to take on the task."

He waved a hand dismissively. "You are the queen on the board, Iressa. They are but lesser pieces. After they have proven their worth, we will find a way to sacrifice them and ensure the weapons reach their proper homes in our hands."

She nodded and seemed to accept the answer. It was true, as far as it went. He had no interest in the daggers, only in Fury, so he would be happy to turn them over to her. *As long as she minds her place.*

"Use the distraction of the first leader's death to have

the witch's group launch their attack on the city. Burn it, sow chaos, create anarchy. We will swoop in on the kemana when there is no one left above to defend it, and the denizens will submit, flee, or die. I do not care which but they shall no longer stand in defiance of me. As our final act, we will destroy Stonesreach and send a message to all who dare oppose us."

She laughed. "It is a wonderful vision of the future. I'll do all I can to make it come true. Do you wish to remove the bounties on the humans to keep the field clear for Pesharn and Jarkko?"

"No. Let's leave things as they are. If there's another attack to soften them up, all the better. If not, I am sure our people will be adequate to the task."

She nodded and rose. "I should go and give Sarah her orders."

"Do so. And, Iressa, remind her of the penalties for failure. For her, it won't be death but a return to the World in Between. That should motivate her properly."

The dark witch smiled. "As you wish, Lechnas."

CHAPTER TWENTY-TWO

Sarah flung the statuette with all her strength and it put a dent in the drywall but simply bounced off. Further enraged by its refusal to shatter, she drew her wand and fired thin beams into it, again and again, to first break it to fragments and then to make the separate parts even smaller. Eventually, it was gone, but her rage was not expended. She snatched up an end table, hurled it at a window, and cringed when it bounced off the reinforced glass. The enormity of what she'd almost done swept over her, and she sank onto her couch and shook in frustration and anger.

The insistent pressure that signaled Iressa's desire to speak to her pressed against her mind and for a moment, she considered ignoring the woman. But when she considered the ramifications of that choice, she realized it wasn't to her short- or long-term benefit to alienate the witch. *No, I have to play my role, leading a band of damned incompetents!* She paused to breathe, the mental shouting doing nothing to abate the tension she felt. Finally, she pushed the table away with her feet instead of her magic, then lay down and crossed her hands over her chest, closed her eyes, and accepted her superior's summons.

The world rippled and she appeared in a facsimile of the room in which they'd killed Dreven. Bloodstains were still visible where he'd died, and the knife rested nearby. The walls and floors were carved stone and flickering lanterns provided the illumination. Iressa stood in the center, her hands clasped behind her back and her head down as if she was meditating. Sarah stepped into the room an arm's length away and waited to be acknowledged. She took the time to stare at the bloodstains and remember her former superior's last moments, and it relaxed something inside her. *I bet if I could kill him again, I'd feel much better.*

The other witch raised her head and gazed into her eyes without speaking for several moments. It grew uncomfortable, and Sarah straightened her spine and returned the stare. Iressa broke into a grin and chuckled. "There's the woman I was waiting for. What is vexing you?"

She snarled, "The discovery of the damned traitor among the damned humans. Not that there was one, obviously, I knew that. But the fact that he escaped before I could flay the skin from his flesh and tissues from his bones? That vexes me."

Her superior laughed outright. "You have excellent fire in you. That is a proper response. I'm sorry you missed your revenge, but perhaps we can make it happen in the future. For now, we need to focus only on actions that advance our goals."

"I believe that killing all the humans, right now, would absolutely advance our goals. We are stronger without them and safer without them."

The other woman frowned. "How did the human leader react?"

Sarah snorted. "He apologized profusely for not seeing the traitor in our midst, even though the man was his friend and his own recruit."

"That simply means our enemy played a very good and very deep game. No, we cannot do away with the humans. They will be needed when we attack the city."

She folded her arms. "I disagree. I think we can accomplish it with only the witches and wizards under my command."

Iressa folded her arms in imitation the stance. "And who will absorb the bullets while your people are busy destroying things?"

She thought about that for a second and sighed. "Okay, you're right. They do make excellent cannon fodder."

"And that's exactly how we will use them, have no fear. Now, I have good news for you on several levels. First, additional help is coming to assist in the elimination of your primary foes."

"The two women?"

"Yes."

"Excellent. What kind of additional help?"

"The extremely lethal kind."

She smiled. "You don't mean that you, personally, will accomplish it, do you?"

Iressa chuckled. "No, I already have more than enough on my plate. A couple of my...former colleagues, I guess you'd call them, have been tasked with killing them. The timing is uncertain but it should be soon. No more than a week for the first one."

"That is good news. To be rid of our enemies in such a short time will be a huge boost to our operations."

"Second, when the moment to attack the city comes, I will be there to assist you and I will bring several powerful beings with me."

"Why the help all of a sudden? Not that I'm at all displeased."

"I have reached the end of my patience with the stalemate. It is time to destroy our enemies and the other humans who harbor them. Only then can we begin to progress toward our ultimate objectives."

"And those are?"

"Power, of course. The answer is always power."

Sarah shrieked as she returned to the physical world, Iressa having given her a Dreven-view of the knife driving at her chest before she sent her back into her body. She sat, muttering, "So much to do and so little time before they're killed and things really begin."

Miles away, in her lab at ARES, Kayleigh monitored the live feed from the witch's apartment. She was inordinately happy that they'd pulled Sloan out and all the more so as she listened to the crazy woman's half-conversation. She gave Alfred instructions to copy it to Diana and Cara, then headed to the elevator. Diana was working out of the fifth-floor conference room today and some things begged to be discussed in person.

The tech poured herself a cup of coffee, heavy on the sugar and cream, and refilled her boss's mug of inky black brew. She sat across from her and waited quietly while the other woman finished whatever she was typing into her tablet, pushed it away, and drew the coffee closer and took a grateful drink. "I think you saved me. Somewhere along the way, I fell down a paperwork rabbit hole and lost track of time and space. I might have been here for a caffeineless eternity if you hadn't interrupted it."

Her companion laughed. "I'm glad I could help. Do you have a few minutes to chat?"

Diana rolled her eyes. "For heaven's sake, we got Sloan out. What the hell do you want now, woman?"

"I want to keep our people safe, same as always. This time, though, I'm more concerned about you and Cara."

She frowned. "Why?"

"I overheard Sarah talking to herself—or to whoever she magically speaks with. If I read between the lines correctly, they're planning to escalate their efforts to kill you and Cara, with the goal of doing it sometime in the next week."

"That's ambitious."

"Right? But that's not all. She mentioned 'help' as if she would have some from Oriceran or wherever she goes when she zones out."

"That could be a problem, I suppose, depending on who's coming. But it's good to know. Anything else useful?"

"Yeah." The tech laughed. "Our favorite witch threw one hell of a temper tantrum before she phoned home."

Diana leaned forward. "Really?"

"Yep. She blasted a statue to pieces with her wand and tried to throw a table through the window."

They laughed together, and the boss asked, "What set her off?"

"Sloan. And humans in general, I think."

"I'd say that's outstanding."

Kayleigh took a sip of her coffee. "I wondered if there was a way to exploit that."

"How do you mean?"

"Well, my thought is that if she's emotional, she's less in control. If she's less in control, that's all the better for us. Perhaps we could find ways to put pressure on her and try to make her upset."

Diana pointed at her. "That is an excellent idea. You get a gold star for the day. What do you have in mind?"

"Oh, I'm sure Deacon and I could come up with something. Off the top of my head, I think insects in their base, or maybe bees. Track some of the members and have them picked up by police or by our bounty people if we want to score a double win. You know, stupid stuff that's simply annoying enough to stack up."

"I love this plan. Make it happen. I bet Rath would have some great ideas too."

The tech stood and grinned. "You've got it, boss. I'll get right on it."

CHAPTER TWENTY-THREE

Diana and Rath stepped through the portal into a corner of the basement of Nylotte's shop and she instantly felt the pull of the sword. Fury rested in a weapon stand in the center of the ward rings, which the Drow had told her were kept active at all times since the arrival of the blade. Even through the protective magics, it called to her. Footsteps sounded on the staircase, and both her teacher and Cara descended to join her. Her second in command had her artifact daggers, Angel and Demon, sheathed at her hips. They'd all agreed that having them around but outside the wards for this effort would be a sensible precaution.

She'd chosen a Siouxsie and the Banshees t-shirt for the day, along with her tactical pants and spy boots. The others were also dressed mainly in black. Cara wore an almost identical outfit with a Van Halen shirt, and the Dark Elf had simply donned her usual leather pants and tight black tunic. Rath's t-shirt had a picture of Judge Dredd on it.

Cara broke the silence. "Are you sure you're up for this, boss? It's not like the thing expires if you wait a while."

"True, but it's beyond stupid to have a powerful ally you leave on the bench." She shook her head to clear the slight temptation to put this off for another day.

"Agreed. I'm only doing my job and trying to keep you from being a looney tune."

"You're far too late," Nylotte replied. "She's been looney for as long as I've known her."

Rath agreed. "Totally looney."

Diana put her hands on her hips and glared at them. "So, this is what you two do when I'm not around—think of new ways to insult me? Nice. Really nice." She pointed at the troll. "And you, the greatest traitor of all." He laughed and she smiled at him. The banter no doubt did the same thing for the others as it did for her, providing a way to not focus on the enormity of the task ahead. The real wounds Cara had taken from the daggers when she fought to master them were at the forefront of her mind, alongside the acknowledgment that a greatsword would cause a much bigger injury if the same scenario occurred. She was heartened to see the array of potions that waited on a bench outside the circular protections.

Her teacher gestured, and the outermost magical ring deactivated. "Well, there's no time like the present, protege."

After a single decisive nod, she drew a deep breath and stepped across the line. The power sprang to life behind her and the circle before her fell. She took another step, and only the center barrier now remained with two layers of defenses behind her. It vanished, and she lowered herself carefully to the lotus position behind the frame that supported the weapon, careful not to accidentally brush the metal. Her own mental barriers were as strong as she could make them, and she resolutely pushed aside all her fears that she might not be up to the task. She had won the sword fair and square, and its former owner had not seemed to be an intellectual giant. Hopefully, whatever lay inside the weapon would consider her an upgrade.

She realized she was stalling when the mental image of herself appeared and tapped her foot, her arms folded and head shaking. *Fine. Let's do this.* She stretched her hand tentatively to touch the sword, and the world exploded in shards of bright light and radiant color and thrust her into an endless fall into the void.

Cara had described the arid and cracked landscape on which she'd battled the daggers, and Diana had imagined her test would take place in the same arena. When her vision returned and she became aware of her surroundings, it was clear her assumption had been utterly wrong. She sat in the center of a gorgeous garden, where gravel-filled paths meandered between sections of carefully manicured trees, bushes, and flowers. She rose gracefully to her feet and turned in a slow circle, taking it all in. A crunching sound behind her caught her attention and she pivoted to discover a young man, probably in his early teens, standing before her. His shoulder-length black hair lay against his pale skin, and his eyes were a shade of blue she'd never seen before. He wore simple sandals, white pants, and an ebony button-down tunic that ended in an upright collar.

He bowed, and not knowing how else to respond, she did the same in return. A grin broke out on his face. "Welcome to the test, bearer."

She nodded. "Are you my foe in this place?"

His laugh was innocent and joyful. "No, I am not. I am only a shadow of the past sent to escort you forward and prepare you for the rite to come." He gestured at a path, and she stepped beside him as he walked ahead. "As you are already aware, Fury can only be transferred with the death of the former bearer. However, simply gaining possession of the blade does not give you access to its power. That must be won separately."

She nodded. She knew that much from Cara's experience. "How about a game of checkers? I'm reasonably good at that."

He laughed again. "If such things were possible, Fury's soul would be far less burdened with the deaths of those who have tried and failed to master him."

Okay, that's kind of a dark thing for someone who's not in high school yet to say. "How are you connected to the sword? Was your, uh, life, trapped inside the artifact as well?"

Her guide pointed to a side path and preceded her onto it with a shake of his head. "Oh, no. There is only one essence inside the blade. However, it has been present long enough that separate parts have splintered to address various needs. I am one of those parts, a memory of the warrior's childhood."

"The warrior? The person who was placed into the sword?"

"Yes."

She swallowed hard and asked before she could convince herself not to. "Was he...I mean...were you a volunteer?"

The boy nodded as if the question was no more or less serious than an inquiry about the weather would have been. "We were. It was a great honor to be chosen. We fought many battles before being considered for the transformation and many more to earn the right to be the one."

She expelled the breath she'd held. "That is a relief. I am glad to hear it."

He nodded. "You might wish that we were less, though, when the trial begins."

"May I ask you about the trial?"

"That is not my purpose. You should wait to meet the warrior himself for that."

"Okay. I can understand that."

The path led to an archway of dark wood comprised of two supports plus a curved lintel. It was engraved with runes she couldn't read and green vines snaked around the top and dangled from the crosspiece. Beyond it, the trail continued and curved to the right. He stopped, stepped forward, and turned to face her. "You have reached the moment of decision, bearer. Some who come this far discover they do not have the fortitude to continue, knowing their life will be at risk. If you wish, we can simply proceed along the path and it will bring you back to your home unharmed. This is your final opportunity to choose that route, however. Should you decide to pursue the power of the sword, you will win or you will die—both here and in your world." He spoke softly. "And it has not, in the past, been a good end for those who have failed but one filled with agony and regret."

"You're quite the salesman."

He laughed. "I do what I was made to do, bearer, and nothing more."

She closed her eyes and considered the options. *Is the sword essential to defeating the Remembrance? Probably not.* ARES had an arsenal of guns and bullets and could bring more people in if necessary. She'd be lying to herself if she said it was only about doing the job. *Do I need the power it offers?* That question was harder. Deep inside, the urge to excel at her magic drove her as hard as anything in her life ever had. The weapon would be a major step forward in that arena, one she was unlikely to be able to duplicate on her own. *Is it enough that I want it to keep it out of the hands of bad people?*

Mental Diana flickered into view, laughed at her, and said, *"Oh, so noble,"* before she vanished. *Okay, fair enough, that's merely an excuse. So why do I really want the sword?* In the end, it was the same answer as she'd given to every challenge she'd faced in her life and career. *I want to be everything I can be, which means facing every challenge that presents itself, no matter how frightening it might seem.*

The young man must have sensed that she'd reached a decision. "Your choice, bearer?"

She opened her eyes and gazed at him with a smile. "I didn't come all this way to back out now."

He turned and brushed several of the runes with his fingertips and they immediately glowed. When he crossed the path and did the same on the opposite support, the area formed by the structure began to glow as well. The continuation of the trail vanished, replaced by a misty golden view of an undefined space. She couldn't help herself and walked forward to peer around the side of the post and look behind the arch. The path continued ahead. She drew back and saw the rich haze and the unknown space behind it, which was definitely not the same as what was on the other side. He pointed forward. "To continue the trial, you must pass through the portal. I will not accompany you further."

Diana sighed. "Thank you for your guidance thus far. Do you have any tips?"

"I have escorted many challengers to this point." Her guide smiled." Some have selected the easy path and returned to their lives unharmed. I always wondered how they would be able to live with themselves, having discovered themselves lacking when offered such an opportunity. Others have continued and succeeded or failed as their own natures demanded. The only truth I have to share is that those who are honest with themselves—who truly know who they are and what they desire—seem to fare better than those who do not."

She placed a fist in her open palm and bowed to her escort, who returned the gesture with his own fluid motion. "That is an entirely useful perspective. Thank you." He nodded and she stepped forward into the golden haze, hoping she was truly as ready for the battle to come as she thought she was.

CHAPTER TWENTY-FOUR

The golden mists parted as Diana walked through them and the garden vanished behind her as she emerged into what was undoubtedly the most beautiful dojo she had ever seen. It was classically Japanese, with ornamental bamboo mats covering the floor in an intricate pattern, a peaked roof several stories above, and white panels all around that permitted light to diffuse into the room. Every structural piece was dark wood, identical to that in the arch that had led her there, but instead of engravings, the surfaces were polished until they shone.

The space was rectangular and the front was one of the short sides, indicated by the presence of an ornamental sword holder. In it lay a representation of Fury, the greatsword unsheathed and shining in the ebony frame. On the floor before it knelt a figure in a grey tunic and a black skirt spread out around him. The being had long, straight black hair gathered in a high knot like a ponytail, and she could see the curve of bangs falling to the side of its face. The voice was deep and resonant, providing the first clue to the figure's gender. "Welcome, bearer."

She advanced slowly until she was beside the man and knelt, keeping her eyes forward on the sword. It was purer and sharper than she recalled from the previous battle, the blade shining silver with ebony runes on it and the hilt wound with beautiful leather. The crossguard appeared simultaneously too ornamental to function and strong enough to stop any attack. There was a sense of potential from it, of power and violence and purity that simply awaited a direction in which to act. "Thank you. I don't know what to call you."

His grin was visible in the corner of her eye. "Fury will do."

"Did you choose that name or was it chosen for you?"

"I was given the privilege of selecting it prior to my transformation."

"And you truly were a volunteer?"

He nodded quickly. "I was. It was a great honor at the time, one I coveted with all I was. Not only did I willingly make the choice, I fought for the right to do so. I endured countless battles to prove my worth as a champion, then countless more to defeat the other champions."

A shiver ran through her. "To the death?"

His voice revealed the presence of a smile. "Only the initial battles. Champions killing one another would have weakened our master's power base. Those matches were sport but no less vicious for it. There were deaths, despite his admonition to avoid it. The prize was immeasurable to us. Immortality in recognition of prowess. What warrior could ask for more?"

"Did you make the right decision?"

"I do not concern myself with such questions. I made a decision and I live with the results. Sometimes, I have a wielder who is attuned to the sensibilities I held when I was alive and I am content to help them. At other times, the match is not as appealing and I am content to wait until the sword changes hands again."

She forced herself not to look at him, despite her desire to know more—to know everything she could before the test to come. "What sensibilities are those?"

He finally turned to her and a smile graced his handsome face, which was unlike any combination of features she'd seen before. Elegant, surely, with fine cheekbones and gorgeous eyes but not quite Elven and certainly not human. "Ah, bearer, that would be telling."

Diana laughed and he did as well. With a nod, she asked, "What can you tell me about the trial to come?"

Fury rose to his feet and she followed suit. He turned, faced the dojo, and gestured at the walls. "It will happen here. There are no rules, although honorable conduct is always preferred. If you are able to defeat me, you will earn the right to wield the full power of the weapon. If you are not able to defeat me, you will almost certainly die."

"It's not guaranteed?"

He shrugged. "I know very little of what happens in your world, so I have no way to know if you can survive the damage you would take in losing in combat. It does not seem likely to me, but I hesitate to say it is entirely sure."

"That makes sense. I appreciate your clarity."

He inclined his head, then swept his arms wide. A shimmer flowed over the space and when it cleared, weapons and shields hung from every surface. Many of them she recognized but some were utterly unfamiliar. She wandered slowly past them and examined her options. Fury did not pressure her. In fact, he seemed as if he would willingly wait for an eternity. She ran her fingers along the dull edge of a wicked-looking scimitar and asked, "So, I have to choose?"

His skirt swished as it brushed against the mats when he walked toward her. "That weapon would be an interesting choice, but no, you do not have to choose. You may select any of these weapons at any time. Of course, unless you wish to face me unarmed, you will have to make an initial selection." The warmth and humor in his voice sounded inclusive rather than oppositional, and she found herself smiling. *Holy hell. The sword is charming.*

She faced him and clasped her hands behind her back, feeling far less formal than she'd like in her concert t-shirt. "And what weapon will you use?"

He smiled. "The rules limit me to only my body and the sword." He gestured to the mammoth weapon at the front of the room.

"It seems like all these options would give me an advantage."

"Appearances can be deceiving."

A nugget of worry began to grow in her stomach as she considered the upcoming combat. "Is magic permitted?"

He raised an index finger and inclined it slightly in her direction. "Ah, excellent. It is always most pleasurable to face an opponent with both martial and magical skills. Yes, magic is permitted, but there is a caveat. Its use will drain you at a much faster rate than it would beyond these walls.

Also, magic and physical strength are fused here as if it is a single large pool that you draw from rather than two energies, as I have previously heard it described."

Dammit. She considered his words and nodded. "That is a good way to describe it. Just so I'm sure, you're saying that using my magic will make me physically tired and drain the same resources I use to swing a sword."

"It is so."

"It hardly seems fair."

"That is not a concern in this place. Only your will and the physical and mental strength to see that will realized." Again, he smiled. "But I am also bound by the same strictures."

"Do you have magical abilities?"

His smile stretched into a wide grin. "Not as such."

She laughed. "You know, for someone who will try to kill me, you're quite entertaining."

"You also." He straightened his already perfect posture into a formal stance. "Are you ready?"

Diana closed her eyes and turned inward, searching for any weakness in her will and in her desire for what was to come. When she opened them again, she knew she was ready and would hold nothing back in her pursuit of victory. "I am prepared."

Fury nodded, turned, and walked without haste to the front of the room where he lifted the greatsword from its holder with both hands and touched his forehead to the blade. He strode to the middle of the dojo and stopped two paces back from the exact center which she now noticed was marked with a small emerald dot on one of the bamboo mats. Her opponent held the weapon horizontally across his body while he waited and again, seemed utterly unconcerned with the passage of time.

She circled the room once more to examine the instruments of death hung on the walls. After the damage she'd taken from the weapon in the previous battle, selecting a shield and going strength-to-strength was not even an option. Each block would risk another bone break if he was as strong as her last opponent, and she was quite convinced that his lithe form hid prodigious power. *After all, he's a champion among champions. Shit. This will be almost impossible.* She pushed the thoughts away with an image of Daffy Duck ramming Bugs Bunny into his hole, yelling, "down down down, go go go, mine mine mine." With a smile, she selected the three weapons she'd liked most in the first pass—a katana and matching tanto with crimson hilts and a dagger, just in case. She slipped the latter into the back of her belt and twirled the other two, the katana in her right hand and the shorter blade in her left. If she'd faced a lighter weapon, she would have preferred to use the sword two-handed, but she would have to rely on speed and agility in the battle to come rather than raw power.

Her choice made, she stepped into place opposite him and he nodded his approval of her selection. "For some bearers—the ones I like—there is a final opportunity to refuse the rite and leave in peace. I will not offer this to you, however, as I know already you will not accept."

She nodded. "I believe we understand one another."

"Then let us begin."

CHAPTER TWENTY-FIVE

F ury flowed forward smoothly and Diana realized that not being able to see his legs beneath his skirt would be a hindrance. *So that's why they wore that. Huh.* Her moment of revelation was truncated when the sword slashed downward at an angle from her left. She stepped toward it and circled the katana to shove the blade away in the direction in which it already moved, then stabbed inward. He made a slight adjustment where their weapons touched and her own attack was easily pushed aside before he disengaged and began to circle slowly.

The only sounds were their breathing, the swish of his skirt on the mats, and the muted crunch of her boots as she moved. The blades rang against one another again as she tried a sequenced attack. The katana swept in from the side to be blocked by the greatsword, and the tanto stabbed forward an instant later. He quick-stepped with his back foot, adjusted his posture, and the attack found only air. His counter-assault whistled at her thighs and she backed away in a rush to avoid it. He turned the swipe into a second attack by spinning in the same direction, this stroke aimed at her head. She batted it up at an angle with the katana and thrust at him with the smaller weapon again, but he skipped out of range, inviting her to over-commit and pursue.

Instead, she retreated, content with what she'd learned of his abilities so far and nervous about what he might have gleaned of hers. They stalked in a circle and studied one another warily for a few moments before he lunged directly toward her. He anticipated her sidestep, moved with her, and brought the sword down at her head. Her only option was to get low, so she let herself collapse backward and drove a heel kick at his groin. It didn't connect but it did force him to retreat a step. Diana spun on her back, flipped into a crouch, and extended a leg to sweep his feet from beneath him, but he simply hurdled the strike. She deflected the angled chop with which he retaliated, veered to the outside, and slashed with her own blades.

They circled again and his expression suggested that he was done with the pregame, as was she. She waded in rapidly and attempted to close the distance so he couldn't use the length of the sword against her. He backpedaled but didn't match her speed and she was able to move inside the weapon's range. The trap was revealed when he lashed out with a front kick that interrupted her charge, hurled her back, and stole her breath. Fury advanced instantly and sliced the weapon downward. She thrust the first blow aside with her katana and managed to deflect the second with the shorter blade. He tried another kick and she spun away, gasping as her body remembered how breathing worked.

Her adversary didn't slow his assault. The sword swiped horizontally and she parried it with a downward stroke with her katana and stabbed at his throat with the tanto. He released his blade with one hand and slapped her wrist away, then threw a backfist at her face. She blocked with the hilt of her sword and enjoyed the brief grimace of pain that flickered across his face at the impact. Her attempt at a follow-up kick to his knee failed when he stepped back to avoid it before he pistoned that leg out in an attack aimed at the nerve bundle in her thigh. She brought the pommel of her katana down on his knee, drove the kick away, and slashed with the blade. He smiled as he swung the greatsword at a strange angle. Her arm tingled alarmingly when her sword shattered in her hand. He instantly reversed the flow and hacked at her, but she stumbled away and snatched the closest weapon she could find.

It turned out to be the scimitar she'd admired earlier. The grip was snug in her fist and she yanked it off the wall in time to block the next blow, using the curved weapon to redirect it. For an instant, he lost his balance and the blade whipped out to score a strike on his upper arm. The grey tunic darkened immediately as his blood flowed.

Fury stepped back and raised his sword in a salute, his blade raised before his face. "You have been a worthy opponent, bearer. I hope that when you reach your species' afterlife, you are received with all appropriate honor." His moves became sinuous, flowing, and completely different than the direct style he'd used thus far. One of Rath's favorite lines popped into her head. *I know something you don't know. I am not left-handed.* Apparently, her foe had concealed his true nature. He whirled the sword in a figure-eight and switched it deftly from hand to hand as if the weight wasn't a concern at all. It was as if she now battled an entirely new person and she was already tired from the first. *That is so not fair.*

He charged and swung the sword with his right hand. Diana blocked it with the scimitar, spun away to try to get inside his guard, and stabbed at his thigh with the tanto. Before she could complete the action, his other fist hammered against her temple and pitched her forward and away from him. She flung herself into the dive, lost her scimitar in the process, and managed to stay barely ahead of his mighty blade. She feinted to one side and ran to the other to gain a little space and turn in the right direction again. He strode slowly toward her and whirled the sword in the damned figure-eight, and she grasped her backup dagger with a sense of growing despair. *He's like the terminator or something. Bloody hell.* He left her no time to get a new weapon, and she didn't know what else she would choose if he did. *Maybe a spear. I could simply throw stuff at him for all the good this has done me.*

Diana angled away as he swiped at her and deflected the weapon away with precise sweeps of her shorter blades. She darted in and managed to cut him in the abdomen, but the sword caught her as she spun and carved a line of fire down her back. A scream of rage escaped at the sudden pain, but the clarity helped her to pierce the fog in her brain. *Damn him. He played me. He made me think about the negatives of using magic so I'd fight him where he was strongest, afraid to weaken myself. Let's see who has the bigger reservoir, then.*

She wore a fierce grin as she turned to him and saw the uncertainty flicker in his eyes in response. A part of her thought it was unlikely he would have lied to her and there probably was a significant cost to using magic in this space. *Okay, then, we'll keep it small.* Blood dripped warmly down her body and knew she didn't have all that much time. At the same time, she also knew that to overextend would cause her to lose the battle and her life. She resorted to her first magic and what she was most comfortable with. When he advanced with another whirling attack, she side-stepped and flicked her fingers to unleash a force blast to nudge the weapon slightly off its trajectory. With her other hand, she grasped the heel of his leading leg with her telekinesis and hauled it forward enough to compromise his balance. She whipped the right-hand blade at his head and he ducked, but the tanto plunged into his thigh before he could recover and retreat.

He limped away but began to circle and swung the sword. "Tiring, like I promised, isn't it?"

Diana nodded. In truth, it felt like she'd been on the verge of tearing something inside her simply to summon that much. But she wasn't sure how much of that was real and how much of it was simply worry planted by his words. *Either way, it doesn't matter. I have to end this.* She thought back to some of her earliest battles against magicals and saw her path forward. When he attacked again, she chose the moment of transfer from one hand to the other in his weaving pattern and yanked at the sword with her telekinesis, whipped it out of his weakened grasp, and hurled it to the side. A mixture of surprise and approval burned in his eyes as she lunged at him, leading with the blades. He fought hard to block her attacks and respond with punches and kicks but ultimately, the little incisions she'd managed to score added up. She plunged the tanto through his right triceps from below, disabling that arm, and spun backward in a crouch to backhand the other dagger into his opposite side ribs when he convulsed.

Fury fell and she collapsed beside him. Blood pooled under him as he smiled at her. All anger and sadness left his face, replaced by carefree happiness. "You are worthy, wielder. I look forward to speaking to you again."

The dojo faded slowly around her and she returned to her body. She lay face-down in the center of the ward rings, and Cara and Nylotte pressed on her back—which she suddenly realized hurt an incredible amount. Her gasp alerted them that she had returned, and the Drow turned her over while her second in command poured a healing potion down her throat. She screamed as the flesh and skin knitted itself together and moaned in relief when the pain faded. Her teacher helped her to stand, and Cara whistled. "Wow, boss, nice scar you've got there."

The Dark Elf leaned around her to study it. "A fitting memento of a battle with an artifact. Since you're here, you must have won?"

Diana nodded and Cara said, "If you need further evidence, there it is." She turned to find the other woman pointing at the weapon holder, where the greatsword had vanished and been replaced by a katana with a black blade and red runes. There was no question that it was still Fury, however. *So my initial choice mattered more than I thought, I guess.* She heard the weapon's laughter in her mind as her hand closed over the hilt.

Nylotte said, "Congratulations, my students. You've accomplished what few before you ever have. But don't forget, this is the start of the fight, not the end."

She sighed, wishing she could argue but knowing she couldn't. Strength flowed into her from the sword as if it, too, knew there were battles to come. "Then I guess we'd better get to it."

CHAPTER TWENTY-SIX

Deacon's home computer rig was adequate for gaming but was nowhere near the level of technology required for his work tasks, which was why he was at ARES headquarters in the middle of the night. Cans of Coke, partially consumed and then forgotten, littered the table behind his workstation. His lab was dark except for the glow from his monitors—five across with the giant one in the center. The outermost displayed surveillance images from the watchers roaming the city, mainly because he found it relaxing to watch the urban landscape gliding by. The inner screens beside these held data he might need as he worked on his current task.

On the big monitor was a display that no one at ARES besides him would be able to see. His magic converted code to images when he so desired, and he'd pictured the firewall of the National Guard system as a giant bank vault, specifically the model from the star-studded remake of *The Italian Job*. The film was among his favorites, despite the fact that he wouldn't be caught dead in a Mini Cooper. He spun a chopstick in his free hand, an expensive lacquered scarlet fidget toy that helped him center his mind. A while back, he'd given the other half of the pair to Kayleigh, but she hadn't adopted his habit yet.

He returned it to the cylindrical black vase that served as its holder with a soft click and lowered his hands to the keyboard. His eyes defocused as he let the image fill his senses, and his magic controlled his fingers and voice to input the code that was the real-world translation of his virtual actions. He unpacked a large drill from the case that appeared at the side of his computer self and set the device up in an instant, a feat that would never be possible in reality. As he pushed the bit forward into the metal of the safe, he watched carefully and focused on the vibrations traveling up to his hands. He killed the power with a kick of the emergency disconnect foot switch when he felt the inner glass shield crack, exactly like in the movie. *As expected, but it had to be tried.*

The tech sighed and his virtual self pressed his ear to the door directly above the dial. Unlike the normal version in the film, there were a thousand hashes on this wheel representing the difficulty of cracking the secure military network. In the real world, his head turned to scan the data on his side monitors, where he had displayed likely passwords and hacking routines to extract more of them. In the virtual representation, a list of numbers appeared in grease pencil on the safe, waiting to be tested. None of them resulted in the click of a pin falling into place, which was frustrating but not unexpected. *No one said it would be easy. It's not the Worthington 1000, after all.*

His fingers danced as he tried known exploits, represented on the screen as spins of the dial. He had proxy-protected access into the best hacking sites on the dark web, as well as a legitimate connection to governmental discussion boards on the topic. All told, he wasn't worried about whether or not he'd be able to crack it given the resources he had at hand. With enough time, he had yet to find the system that could stand against him. But since he hadn't been invited in the front door of the network, the possibility of triggering an alarm that would start a clock running on the operation was high despite his skill.

Fifteen minutes later, the first click rewarded his perseverance. Once he'd discovered one, the rest revealed themselves more quickly. Finally, the safe was unlocked and he yanked the handle down with a smile to access the goods inside. He heard the snap of the failsafe and cursed. *That is a stupid amateur trap, and I fell for it.* Deacon grasped the papers held within, which translated to dumping data into local storage in the real world. He finished quickly, rose, and turned to discover that the door he'd used to enter the room had vanished. *From the Italian Job into The Matrix. Dammit.* He cast about for a weak part in the wall that would represent a way to get whatever software was seeking him off his back and found the place he needed. A sharp kick broke the seal, and the hidden door flew open to reveal a circle of police officers with their guns aimed at him. He raised his hands, quipped, "Howdy, boys," and dissolved from the virtual space.

In the real world again, he checked to ensure his trail was secure and was pleased to discover they hadn't even made it past the first proxy server. He hid his actions behind Chinese IPs, having decided it was appropriate given the espionage they'd discovered had been perpetrated by that country. With a grin, he set the data he'd stolen to scroll on the main monitor so he could review it and leaned back, reached for his can of Coke, and grimaced. It had, like all the others, gone warm while he was working.

Kayleigh laughed when Deacon finished describing his hacking attempt on the National Guard base. She always enjoyed hearing how his magic worked over the Internet but she could never really understand it any more than she could make fire come from her fingertips. There had been a time when she was jealous of those with abilities she didn't have, but Emerson had set her straight by reminding her that her brain was something they didn't have and that teams were supposed to have complementary parts.

Diana and Tony arrived promptly for the meeting, and the two techs began by relating the newest information from their surveillance on the oversight committee members, including the new potential names that had come to light. "We found nothing of concern on Finley's but weren't exactly shocked when we discovered some questionable activity on the part of the VP's political buddies."

The boss shook her head with an angry expression. "That really is unfortunate. I'd hoped he'd be smart enough to avoid it."

Tony shrugged. "We all did. But it's not the first time a

politician has gotten his priorities confused. Maybe it'll work out."

Kayleigh doubted it but didn't voice her opinion. "So, in addition to that, we've worked to push Sarah to a new level of frustration and I have to say, it's been way more fun than I expected it to be."

Deacon laughed. "Totally awesome, really. I think we could probably go pro at this."

The investigator grinned. "So, tell us."

The blonde tech was proud of what they'd accomplished so far and was more than willing to share. "First, we made sure her condo has rolling brownouts that strangely coincide with when she's home."

Her partner nodded. "We've tried to catch her in the elevator, but that system is totally local so we can't hack the interior cameras. Maybe we'll send Rath in with an access point."

"Evil plan," Diana said with a grin. "I love it. What else?"

Kayleigh laughed. "Bugs—real and virtual—at the warehouse. Rath put a box of crickets in the ventilation system, and we opened it remotely when he was gone. They hated that, although it didn't take the magicals long to kill them all. Plus, they'll find more listening devices the next time they do a sweep to remind them they're not operating in secret."

"We've also had a few of them picked up by hacking the police bounty system," Deacon added. "When we have enough info on someone to isolate them, we throw their name on there. It's a random tactic but useful. Unfortunately, our security agency hasn't been available to make the arrests."

Tony shrugged. "They're busy with ARES stuff." Diana nodded.

Kayleigh took the briefing over again. "Those have been good, based on what we've heard her ranting about in her apartment. But what's really setting her off are the rumors. Sloan is going—disguised with illusions—to all their hangouts and spreading bad stuff about the gang, claiming they're led by a crazy person, that they keep getting beaten by the police, and whatever other derogatory comments he can come up with. She doesn't like that at all."

Their boss frowned. "That doesn't seem like a particularly safe thing to do."

The tech nodded. "I told him that. His response was, and I quote, 'Darlin, this is what I do.' Honestly, he's infuriating. Finally, he's out, and here he is, putting himself in danger again."

Tony tapped his finger on the table and looked thoughtful. "Is there a way to amp that up a little?"

She turned to face him. "Like what? Deacon and I can probably put something out on the web, too—rumor-wise, I mean."

"No, I was thinking of something a little bigger. What if, instead of simply spreading random rumors by word of mouth, we involved a few officials? If the chief of police talked about the gang and positioned them as simply another group of criminals, that would be sure to tick the magicals off. Even better, if we could convince them to announce they were considering forming a task force, that would surely make Sarah nuts."

Diana looked thoughtful. "That's definitely a way to up

the ante on what we're already doing. Do you think it puts the police in an unnecessary amount of danger, though?"

He shook his head. "That's what they're paid to do. But no, I don't think it does. If we continue to run surveillance on them, we can scream a warning if it looks like they'll make a move. We know that things are moving toward a final action on their part and if we can't head it off at the very least, it would be good to push them into moving prematurely—into acting emotionally rather than logically."

She stood quickly. "It's a good plan. Make it happen. Let's put all the pressure we can on them and be ready for something to break. Tony, after you talk to the PD, get with Hank and Anik and double-check that we're prepared to move on a moment's notice. Kayleigh, spread rumors on the internet. Deacon, try to find us a way to replace the inside knowledge we lost when Sloan jumped ship. I'd start with watchers positioned overhead or in a continuous pattern. Maybe it's possible to put better video and microphones on them? Heat sensors?"

The two techs exchanged glances before they nodded at the same time. Kayleigh said, "We'll think of something."

The worry on their boss' face was a reminder that despite the joy of playing pranks on the group, the stakes were far higher than anyone would like. Once Diana and Tony had left, she leaned in to whisper to Deacon, "So, are we good for the other plan?"

He nodded. "We have full access to all their systems, although I don't know how long it'll last once we go visible. I'm not doing anything other than avoiding detection and sneaking in deeper when the opportunity presents itself."

"It doesn't sound like there's much more we can do on that front."

"Agreed."

"This is probably a one-shot, right?"

"Almost certainly. If it were me and I found out that such a vital system had been compromised, I'd sever external connections entirely. If they do that, we're toast unless we physically break in and add our own hardware."

She frowned. "Do you think we could do the same thing we did with the PD drones? Have the National Guard ones go missing long enough to alter them?"

"No chance."

"Dang it."

He laughed. "You've been hanging around Rath too much if that's all the verbal venom you've got."

Kayleigh grinned. "Shut the hell up or you'll see what I've got."

Deacon raised an eyebrow, which earned him a slap on the arm. "Get to work, slacker." She called her systems up and began to play with the specs for the watcher drones. *Now, if we replaced the standard camera with a heat sensor and used two of them in tandem....*

CHAPTER TWENTY-SEVEN

Pesharn looked at her two lieutenants, then at two humans she had paid to assist in the assassination. "Are there any questions?" Her fellow warriors shook their heads but as expected, one of the locals decided to speak.

"So, to be clear, you want us to run her down, is that it?"

The Kilomea hid her exasperation. They'd been over this twice already. Part of her imagined that the witch, Iressa, had deliberately connected her with the dumbest members of this planet's native species. "Yes. When I give you the signal that she's left her workplace, you are to crash into her motorcycle with your cars, if you can. The two of you will work together to herd her in a certain direction at the same time in case you can't catch her."

One of them smacked the other on the sleeve and laughed. "Some chick on a bike will actually outrun us? Like hell." The two were of a type with their flannel shirts, dirty jeans, cowboy boots, and worn leather jackets proclaiming membership in some group. She found them irritating at best and worthy of a long torturous death the rest of the time. *Well, if they fail me, at least I can make that vision a reality.*

Her male lieutenant growled, and she touched him gently on the arm. "She has proven slippery before and, in fact, evaded several highly reputable bounty hunters. If you are able to kill her, so much the better—and you will be doubly rewarded for it. If not, we will be there as a backup plan."

They nodded and took the hint from her subordinate's attitude that further questioning wouldn't be appreciated. "Okay. We'll get into position and wait for your call."

The men departed, and her female lieutenant shook her head. "You don't actually believe they will manage to kill this human woman, do you?"

Pesharn chuckled. "It is virtually impossible, but stranger things have happened. Is the trap in place?"

She nodded. "Everything is ready."

"Very well. Iressa's subordinates are watching the building that the fools still think is secret. She was seen entering, and they will inform us the instant she leaves."

"What if she uses her magic to travel?"

A low growl escaped her. "She is our prey and one way or another, we will have her. She can't stay hidden from our spotters forever, and when she reveals herself, we will strike."

Cara threw a final rifle to Hank, having disassembled and cleaned it after running a hundred test rounds through it. The new gear was going into the mobile armory, and she'd offered to help wherever she could. Getting paid to shoot was kind of a bonus in any case, and her often frantic mind enjoyed the quiet focus of equipment maintenance. It was one of the things she shared with the former aircraft mechanic, and they had spent many hours together like this since their first introduction.

"Dinner?" he asked,

She shook her head. "Nope, gotta get home and hit the sack." *With Anik, unless something has gotten in the way of our plans again.*

He shrugged, unoffended. "Your loss. I'll try the fondue place. I hear it's really good stuff."

"Well, if anything could tempt me, sizzling steak is the thing, but no, I'm beat." She waved goodbye as she retrieved her helmet and headed to the parking garage. Her replacement bike wasn't as amazing as her Arch had been, but she still enjoyed the way the emerald Kawasaki Ninja H2 cornered, and its acceleration was nothing to sneeze at, either. She didn't have the same instinctive symbiosis with it that she'd had with her own, but it was a good temporary solution until her name came up on the waiting list.

She accelerated out of the garage and turned right, then zig-zagged onto a street leading into the city's up-and-coming neighborhoods. Gentrification had spread and she was a beneficiary, having found a decent apartment on the edge of one of the coolest. She took the back way, which meandered through old industrial complexes, rather than deal with the traffic that was already fairly backed up for a weeknight. The streetlights fell away, and only the mainte-nance and security lamps on the abandoned buildings offered a glimmer of light as she drove along an access road that had once served a steel mill. She realized that she'd vaguely heard the thrum of another engine under the sound of her own only when Quinn's warning eclipsed them both. "Two cars appear to be exceeding the speed limit and heading in your direction."

Cara cursed. While the route provided the advantage of a lack of traffic, it also presented very few options. "Show me." An overlay map appeared on her display. One of the vehicles came up fast from behind and the other could most likely cut her off at the next intersection. She gunned the engine, and the bike surged beneath her. The other cars matched her acceleration. "Dammit, they must have eyes on me."

"Agreed."

"Okay, you know the drill. Full alert to ARES in case this is part of a bigger action. Be ready to roll ambulances if necessary. Plot police presence so I can avoid dragging them into this." She and Diana had concurred on that point. Even though the local authorities were certainly responsible for protecting the safety of their citizens, it didn't seem right to ask any of them other than the SWAT teams to get involved with the Remembrance goons. They wouldn't reach out to those highly skilled professionals unless and until things were truly dire. *No, this beef is personal and we'll handle it personally.*

She leaned over the handlebars and accelerated even more while she watched the positions of the cars on the map. It seemed she would beat the one ahead to the intersection and had a surprise ready for him. The vehicle behind had gained, though, and the timing required to deal with the other meant she couldn't go any faster. By the time she reached the four-way, he'd only be a few car lengths behind...which actually might turn out to be a good thing. Adrenaline coursed through her, and she realized she was grinning. *All the sneaking around we do is one kind of fun, but balls-out speed is its own reward. Not to mention explosions.*

The scene played out in slow motion in her mind as it occurred and looked for all the world like an action film sequence. She saw the car approach from her left, an old-school Mustang with a thick white racing stripe on the dark hood. It spewed a cloud of dust that floated and drifted in the red illumination from its taillights. She couldn't quite see the driver, but whoever it was had earned his or her fate. The bike swerved a little when she lifted her left hand from the handlebars and extended it, her gloved fingers splayed outward and parallel to the ground. Darts of fire burned through the leather, the first volley barely dispatched before the second followed. She secured her grip on the motorcycle and had an instant to reflect on the fact that, before training with Nylotte, the double attack would have probably exhausted her and resulted in a wreck.

Her aim was true, and the missiles stabbed through the front right tire and into the engine compartment as the car dipped toward the road. The strike caused it to flip when the nose dug into the ground. She was well past before it landed and had a moment of celebration at the sound of crunching metal behind her before she noticed that the second dot was still on her tail. *Dammit. Well, that's one, anyway.* She couldn't make the same attack on the second without losing control, so she twisted the accelerator again and hurtled forward. "Quinn, send an ambulance and a police car."

"Done."

"Okay, what are my options?" The map zoomed out and three paths appeared superimposed in varying shades of yellow. An intersection lay about a mile ahead, and the yellow lines diverged. The first path led right and down to the abandoned steel mill, and while it would be better for her bike than for the car, there was no telling how well-maintained the road would be. The second was a continuation of this street, which ran flat and straight for several miles more and gave her no particular advantage. The third, however, was a twisting and turning affair to the left that climbed one of the area's biggest hills. While she wouldn't manage as much speed as the car might on the incline, the nimbleness of the motorcycle would make all the difference. Plus, all she needed was to get far enough ahead to stop and blast them off the road with her magic. "Good. Onward and upward, as they say."

The map showed the car gaining on her, but her instincts told her she would make it to the intersection before her enemy. The driver must have realized the same thing because there was a bang and a whoosh and suddenly, the dot jumped closer.

"Nitrous boost, apparently," Quinn reported.

"Awesome." She divided her attention between the road ahead, the dots on the display, and the car she could now hear surging up on her left. She leaned forward, drew the Ruger awkwardly from the small of her back, and fired it blindly at the other vehicle, which was now only a single length behind her. It swerved a little in her mirrors but continued to gain. "Dammit." She gritted her teeth and drew on all the speed she could with the intersection only fifteen seconds ahead.

With only ten seconds to go, her pursuer pulled beside her and she could see the grin on the face of the man behind the wheel. Four seconds later, he swerved slightly to the left and she realized what he was about to do. With three seconds to go, he swung to the right and tried to ram her off the road. She veered away and onto the shoulder. The bike juddered over the uneven grass and became momentarily airborne when the incline suddenly dropped away. When it landed, she fought for control and steered back onto the road toward the steel mill. *A little more distance, then I can stop and get ready to blast him.* She tapped the brakes to slow herself without throwing the motorcycle into a skid. "Quinn, give me a better look at where he's—"

She didn't manage to finish the statement as a chain buried in the dirt in front of the bike suddenly raised into the air. It caught the front wheel and hurled her over the handlebars. The flight was painless but the abrupt and painful impact into the side of one of the mill buildings left her dazed and all but unconscious.

CHAPTER TWENTY-EIGHT

Her senses clawed back to reality when a very alarmed Quinn yelled into her helmet. "Cara. Get. Up. Now. Enemies incoming." She stumbled to her feet, her brain not able to process anything other than the pulsing yellow line on her display that told her what direction to move in. The helmet made strange noises and the image in front of her slid in and out of resolution, with static filling her vision in the interim. She fumbled at her belt for the healing potion, one of two she'd carried since discovering the existence of the bounty on her head. Once she had it in her hand, she tried to flip the faceplate up, but it was wedged shut.

"Shit." Speaking hurt like there was glass coating her throat. "Quinn, call for help. Any help. I have to ditch the helmet." She ripped it off without waiting for a reply and drank the contents of the vial. Immediately, her head began to clear, and as the pain slowly faded, she realized exactly how many parts of her body were hurting. She considered taking the second as well but decided there was no way to predict how much worse the situation could get. *I might need it more later.* She pushed ahead, and despite the silence around her, she still felt danger lurking. Since it was a trap, there was doubtless someone moving in to kill her and she needed to get out of the open.

She finally located a door and she shoved it with her shoulder. When it failed to budge, she kicked it and the flimsy lock clicked free and allowed her access. She stood in a high-roofed warehouse that looked like the owners had moved out suddenly and never returned. From the entryway, she could vaguely see what she thought might be forklifts, stacks of crates, piles of random metal pieces, and other debris, no doubt covered in dust and rust. The space was dark, and she put her glasses on to have a better look with the enhanced night vision. They immediately signaled to HQ, and Kayleigh's voice came over the comms. "Cara, Quinn alerted us. What's up?"

She tapped the side of the glasses in the code for "Danger," which encapsulated both her need for assistance and her inability to respond verbally. A scuffling sound to the left caught her attention and she moved ahead and paralleled the short side of the rectangle that made up the building. It stretched some distance on the long sides, and she could see a catwalk above, although she didn't notice anyone up there. She toggled the glasses to heat-sensing mode and found three figures, each of which was larger than human size. Kayleigh fed her the blueprints of the structure, which appeared in the far-right portion of her visual field. There were two other potential exits other than the one she'd entered by, and both were blocked by one of the glowing images. She saw their strategy and knew that those two, at least, would continue forward to pen her in and most likely attack her together. While she couldn't locate any others, she had no doubt that they were there somewhere—perhaps outside, waiting to trap her if she bolted.

Kayleigh whispered, "Help is on the way. ETA nine minutes." Cara shook her head. *There is no way I can hide for that long.* There really was no other option. She would have to go on the offensive. She turned left to creep along the length of the warehouse, one stack of crates and debris away from the wall. The assassin who was now on her left was closer, but if she could eliminate the target ahead silently, she might be able to sneak out of the building without them noticing. She crept quietly toward him but when the one she tried to avoid began to angle in her direction, she realized they could see her, too. *Damn. Okay, secrecy is out.* She drew her Glock from its shoulder holster and ran forward.

In the green-tinted reality of the low-light display, plus the heat signature overlay, the figure in front of her was like something out of a nightmare, and she tapped the button that would remove the extra detection mode. The creature was revealed as the Kilomea she'd guessed it was and lumbered toward her as she ran to meet it. When they were a dozen feet apart, she pulled the trigger and continued to fire. The bullets pounded into its torso, but it rushed onward, apparently undeterred. *Dammit. I'm loaded with anti-magic, not AP, and he has a thick hide.*

There was no time to do anything but react as he swung a giant ax at her head. She ducked beneath it and skittered back, all too aware that one of the beast's partners could be closing from the rear. She thrust the gun into its holster with one hand and fired flaming darts at him with the other. They penetrated, and he staggered before he bellowed with pain and anger and resumed his charge again. With gritted teeth, she blasted him a second time as she raced forward to escape the footsteps that suddenly thundered behind her.

Her adversary fell, and she leapt over his body and tapped to activate the heat signatures again. Cara cut left, then left, then right in an effort to create some distance between her and her pursuer. She couldn't hear the Kilomea anymore, which was far from reassuring, so she paused to assess the situation and turned slowly in a complete circle while she scanned the warehouse for him. A whisper of a breeze triggered her to panic and she leapt instinctively to the side. That was all that saved her as the sword stroke whipped past, barely an inch from her arm. The huge form pounded into her and she fell with a painful, breath-stealing thud. Her glasses shattered on the cement floor and the shards spun away. She barely had time to locate her attacker before she had to roll to the side to avoid the sword again.

The Kilomea smiled at her as she scuttled back and lurched awkwardly to her feet. "You should give up now, tiny creature." The voice was identifiable as a female, even though the two genders weren't really all that different when it came to their species.

Cara brushed dirt from the shoulder of her leather jacket and spat a mouthful of blood to the side. *Talking is good. I wonder how much longer before help arrives.* "It's you who should give up. My people are on the way, they'll be here any second." If only she knew how long she had to wait, but with her glasses destroyed, she was well and truly on her own. Her best estimate gave her about five minutes —way too long in this kind of desperate situation.

"They won't, of course." The assassin laughed. "And even if they were coming, do you truly believe we would have set up our killing field without a plan for them, too?"

She shook her head. "This is our turf, sister. You may be hot stuff on your planet but here, you're merely an over-sized cockroach waiting to be splattered."

Her opponent sighed. "It is better this way." She tossed the sword casually from hand to hand as if daring her to try to escape. There was no question that it was a trap, so she feinted in one direction and dashed in the other when the creature reacted. The swing came late and behind her, and Cara reversed course to dart in as her foe tried to bring the weapon around. She delivered a punch to the Kilomea's face with her full strength behind it, and the massive head snapped back. Almost immediately, she was on the defensive again as the sword chopped viciously at her.

Dammit, they're too strong for fists. Diana's must have been undersized or something. Fortunately, I have another option. Cara had tried not to become too reliant on the daggers, but there was clearly no way she would defeat the brute without their assistance. She snaked her hands to the sheaths hidden under her jacket and drew the weapons to give them a twirl before she positioned herself.

Her flight had deliberately taken her out of the open area at the bottom of the stairs to near the catwalk, as she judged it likely that the third opponent would have chosen the high ground for protection while waiting for the others to tire her out. The female in front of her wore a concerned look now, and it was Cara's turn to grin. "Last chance, sister. Get out of here and live to hunt another day. Stay, and I'll hand you your heart."

The assassin growled and charged, feigning outrage on her face while her motions remained calm and controlled. The daggers whispered in the agent's mind and she followed their instructions to curve Angel in her right hand in an inside-out block that rang against the blade and stabbed Demon at the wrist above the sword hilt. Her foe lowered her arm to avoid the weapon, as expected, and Cara whipped her right-hand dagger up to slash at her face. It cut deep into her cheek, far more damaging than her fists or bullets had been, and the Kilomea backpedaled and swung her sword around in a wicked effort to decapitate her. She ducked and controlled the blade with her left-hand dagger once it had passed, while she snaked Angel in for a blow at the Kilomea's ribcage, which was exposed by the twisting action. It scraped along a bone, denying her the end of the fight she had hoped for, and Cara disengaged and skipped out of her opponent's range.

The creature ran the back of a hand across her face and growled what sounded like a curse. "You'll die for that."

She laughed. "You've been trying to kill me for the last minute or so. What makes you think that'll scare me now?"

Her opponent bared her teeth. "Before, I was playing." She reached around her back and produced a long knife that she held confidently in her right hand. "Now, the time for play has ended."

The massive assailant attacked and even with the

assistance of the artifacts, Cara was hard-pressed to defend against the initial flurry. The blows came at unexpected angles, and she dodged and deflected but could find no opening to counter. She gave ground, knowing each passing second brought the potential for help. All she had to do was last a few more minutes until others would arrive to assist her. She only realized she'd become distracted when the Kilomea's blade slid off a poorly angled block and pierced her stomach. Agony seared through her and she spasmed involuntarily. Her reaction was instinctive. She raised her hand and released darts of fire directly into her enemy's eyes from a distance of mere inches. The giant collapsed and released the sword, and the weapon slid noisily across the concrete.

Cara clawed at the healing potion. Tears streamed from her eyes and her breath refused to come. Her trembling fingers closed on it and she tipped it into her mouth but stopped when she choked. She managed to calm herself long enough to swallow a little, and as it went to work, draining the rest became easier. When the liquid had finished healing her, she could barely move and her body ached like she'd fallen down a mountain although already, the memory of the pain was sliding away. She retrieved the energy potion, and drained it in a gulp, and sighed when the strength surged through her.

"I'm waiting for you, Cara Binot," a voice called from above. It was accompanied by a crash followed by a whooshing sound as the floor of the warehouse erupted into flame. *Dammit, the exits and backup are now both blocked. They really thought this through. Bastards.* She sprinted to the stairs to the catwalk and stopped when she reached the narrow platform. Her opponent stood three-quarters of the way along the one that ran down the center. Behind the Kilomea were windows that would enable Cara to escape the inferno—if she could get to them.

"I don't suppose you'd agree to both of us getting out of here and finishing this outside?"

The assassin laughed and struck her sword—which looked to be a foot longer than the one she'd already faced —against the round shield strapped to her left arm. "I am willing to die to see that you do the same. We can burn together, human. Of course, I believe my hide is thicker than yours, so that may not be the actual outcome."

Cara's magic pulsed in her veins, and delivered a double volley, hoping to end the confrontation before it began. Her adversary brought her shield around to deflect the blasts, and they ricocheted from its surface. "Come now, Cara Binot." Her enemy grinned. "Did you think I was unaware of your powers? I hope you can do better than that."

She wanted nothing more than to get out of the building, which was rapidly filling with smoke, but could see no way to do it other than through her opponent. The creature seemed content to wait her out, true to her words. Cara walked forward slowly as she considered potential strategies and rejected them as fast as they came to mind. A fight on the catwalk would have incredible limitations, especially given the large fireproof shield. She had a spare magazine for the Glock, but the anti-magic rounds wouldn't drive through the tough hide any more effectively than her fire darts had. She considered trying to slide under her foe but discarded that on the assumption that she'd simply be crushed if she tried. It was Demon who gave her the answer. His voice whispered instructions, and Cara's eyes widened in surprise.

"Really?" she said. The creature looked strangely at her, but the internal counsel of her dark guide offered confirmation. *Well, it's not like I have any better ideas right now, anyway.*

She hurtled forward and the smile on her opponent's face indicated her pleasure at the choice. It flickered into uncertainty and then alarm when she hurled Angel at the Kilomea's face. Predictably, the shield came up to protect her features and the dagger continued toward it, a little too high to strike the barrier even if she hadn't raised it. But the objective hadn't been to actually hit, only to cause her to reposition.

Time slowed as Cara focused inwardly to talk to Demon. "So, how do I do this?"

His voice was eager and filled with satisfaction, presumably because she'd chosen to follow his instructions. "First, reach for your flame but do not let it go." She obliged and found the source of her magic easily.

"Okay, now what?"

"Focus it not into your fingers, but into your hand. Stop it before it leaves your palm."

That was more difficult but she had all the time in the world, seemingly, to accomplish it. A portion of the magic refused to obey, and she felt her fingertips warm slightly but most of it stayed where she wanted it. "Done."

"Now, imagine that the dagger is an extension of your hand. Let the magic flow into it but do not allow it to leave. Fill it with your power."

She'd known the artifacts could act as reservoirs of magical energy but had never envisioned them being used in quite this way. Nonetheless, she nudged it in the required direction and was encouraged when it flowed easily into the weapon. *Maybe this was why they supported my choice to stick with only fire magic.*

Demon sounded as pleased as could be. "Now, cut that bitch's shield out of the way."

Time snapped into full speed and she raised Demon in a diagonal slice that carved the metal of the shield in half and delivered a wicked, instantly cauterized gash to her adversary's arm. Angel returned to her hand, and she thrust both weapons forward to stab the stunned Kilomea in the chest. Her foe's eyes widened in disbelief as her blood spurted, and Cara stepped back from the weak sword strike that accompanied the critically wounded creature dropping to one knee.

Her opponent looked up in pain and anger. Unexpectedly, she began to chuckle and blood burbled under the sound. Her words emerged between choked coughs. "For so long...you have thwarted us. Two members of the circle dead...now you have claimed a third." She slumped against the railing, and the agent sheathed her daggers. "When you...finally kill...Iressa and Lechnas... Tell them... Pesharn cursed them...with her...last breath." Her eyes rolled back in her head and she slid off the catwalk into the inferno below.

Cara sprinted toward the windows with flames licking at her heels. She gathered all her strength and leapt out blindly, tumbling amidst the falling shards of glass and hoping someone with a healing potion was waiting below.

CHAPTER TWENTY-NINE

Diana gazed at the two other ARES women in the fading light as afternoon changed to evening. Cara still moved like she was exhausted from the healing potions as she retrieved coffee from the carafe on the credenza. Kayleigh looked as if something continued to chew on her from within, a situation she'd thought was in the past when they'd extracted Sloan from his undercover assignment. She turned to face Rath, who was in the chair beside her at the table in the fifth-floor conference room. "We're quite a mess, aren't we?"

He laughed. "Is hard winning all the time. Better than alternative."

She shook her head as the others chuckled and took their places across from her. "So, the reason I've called you here today is.... Oh, wait, each of you asked to chat to me separately, so I have no idea why we're here. Who wants to go first?"

Kayleigh raised her hand from the table and bent it at

the wrist. *That woman can make anything seem sarcastic.* Diana nodded for her to proceed.

"We had a new take from the witch's apartment late, late last night. Apparently, we've pushed her good and hard, right to the breaking point, with the official announcements about the gang. As always, we only had one half of the conversation, but Deacon and I came to the same conclusion independently. She's calling in the troops —all of them. It started yesterday before the attempt on Cara. She was absolutely crowing about Cara's death, I might add."

"Before? That's interesting."

The other woman spoke. "Maybe they were already preparing to kick the action off once either you or I was out of the picture. You should be extra careful, by the way. That trap was seriously well-crafted. It's good that Tony and Sloan came up with the clever plan to put the word out that it succeeded because I sure don't want to face another episode like that anytime soon." The look in her eyes showed exactly how deeply the experience had affected her. *One more thing to make these bastards pay for.*

"In any case, it's a good bet that something is about to happen," Kayleigh said. "We activated the early warning plan when we heard, so Lady Alayne and Nylotte have both been alerted, as have Bryant, Rath's friend Charlotte Stanley, the chief of police, the SWAT lead, and the National Guard posts nearby."

Diana nodded. It had taken considerable debate to decide who to inform and who not to inform but in the end, they'd made the right decisions. "Is that all?"

The tech shrugged. "Otherwise, more of the same. We're still running surveillances and still finding leaks among those we're supposed to be able to trust. The improved pattern recognition software to give the watchers more autonomy is functioning well, so if they do decide to gather and attack somewhere, we should have as early a warning as it's possible to get."

"Have you come up with any new irritants for the witch?"

She shook her head. "No, we ran out of clever ideas and were working on more when all this happened."

"Okay, good deal." Diana turned to face Cara squarely. "And what did you want?"

Her second in command looked uncomfortable as if she didn't want to say what she had to say in front of Kayleigh but made a visible effort to steel herself. "Boss, no disrespect, but it's time to change our approach to these bastards."

"Okay," she replied levelly. What did you have in mind?"

"Quit waiting and start acting."

"Is this because of the Kilomea?" She was sure it wasn't but wanted the other woman to be clear about her own motivations.

Cara shook her head. "I considered that. No. It's about...well, everything. I had reached this conclusion before coming in here this morning, but what Kayleigh shared makes me even more convinced."

"That sounds serious."

"I think we need to confront the Remembrance now with no more delay and no more screwing around. If they're calling in their reinforcements, it's a chance for the clean sweep we've been waiting for."

Diana paused to think it through. "How should we do it?"

Kayleigh spoke before the other woman could answer. "The warehouse. I can have stun drones nearby in case any try to escape, and it seems like a reasonably easy location to attack. There are way too many corners, sure, but at least there won't be people with rifles shooting at you from a distance."

"Cowards," Cara grumbled.

She clearly hasn't moved past the destruction of her motorcycle. Either of her motorcycles. Diana shook her head. "There are any number of risks there, trying to take them all at once. What about using the stun drones as they roll out to their attack?"

The tech shrugged. "We could do that, but if we miss some, they're already on wheels. This way, the ones who are missed are the ones who get stunned. Besides, what if they decide to portal somewhere instead of driving out of the base?"

She scowled but couldn't argue. "Yeah, that's a concern. How do we make it so it's not us walking into a firing squad?"

Cara grinned. "I have a thought on that. Aerial assault."

Diana frowned. "Did you hit your head when you jumped out of that window? You're making less sense than usual."

Her second in command laughed. "No, really. Helicopter deployment like we did on the train. We land on the roof, blast a few holes, and drop in."

"It would certainly have the element of surprise."

"Plus, it negates their ability to use the building as a defensive position. We'll be on them before they can get it together."

She pictured it in her mind. There was still too much that could go wrong, but it was ambitious enough that it might actually work. With the right amount of planning, they could probably pull it off. She frowned. "What's to keep Sarah from bolting as soon as she hears us come in?"

"I knew you'd see that problem." Cara sighed. "I don't have an answer to that yet."

Kayleigh sounded thoughtful. "You said that at one point, you fought against a guy who could suppress portals, right?"

"Yeah, you're right. I did."

"I bet Nylotte knows how to do that," Cara said eagerly. Do you think she'd join the fun?"

"Couldn't she simply counter all their magic, then?" the tech asked with a frown.

The second in command shrugged. "Hell if I know. But since we've never seen someone do it, I'll go with a big old 'no' on that one."

"I'll have to agree with that, Diana added. "No way. But it's a good idea. I'll find out."

Deacon barged into the room as she said the last words. "Whatever it is you plan to find out, you'd better do it fast. Everyone we're tracking has started to move toward the warehouse. It looks like it's on."

Those present bolted to their feet. Diana pointed at the door. "Deacon, put out the call for our people. Cara, get the mobile armory prepped to roll out as soon as we're all here. Kayleigh, wrangle the helicopter and get the rest of our aerial support in the air." She gestured with her arms to summon a portal. "I'll talk to Nylotte." By the time the others had left the room, she was already in the Kemana.

CHAPTER THIRTY

Diana returned as the others were loading into the truck. She was the last in and triggered the doors to close behind her before took her seat beside Cara at the rearmost set of lockers. "I'm in. Go."

Hank was the driver as they hadn't added a new team member for that task yet. "Welcome back. We're rolling." The mobile armory lurched as it pulled away from the building's loading dock. It was disguised as a delivery vehicle for a large box store at the moment, but the electronic skin could transform its identity at the press of a button. The team had discussed the value of entering one of the city's many tunnels with one look and emerging with another, amused by how much that would mess with anyone trying to track them.

The comms were quiet while everyone focused on getting geared up in the new space. They'd planned a few trial runs, but the way the situation had intensified over the last weeks had preempted them. Diana slipped Fury's carry strap up over her head and hung the weapon in its sheath on a locker hook. Another of the many things they hadn't yet managed to find a solution for was a convenient way for her to carry the damn thing when she wasn't in full kit. *Ah, well, first things first. We'll destroy these idiots once and for all, then there will be time to deal with all that.*

She stripped her civilian clothes off and packed them away and slipped on the black ARES base tunic, her tactical pants, and high combat boots. The black uniform top went next, and the utility belt clipped on over it all. Rath acted as a runner since he had geared up faster than the others and delivered two flash-bang grenades and two sonics, which she divided between her thigh strap and belt. She transferred the Ruger from the boots she'd worn when she'd entered the vehicle to its holster off-center at the small of her back.

Kayleigh's voice overrode the sounds around her as Diana worked her way into the bulletproof and at least temporarily magic-proof vest. "The chopper will meet you halfway there. They'll have ropes but you'll have to bring the magnets from the truck."

"Affirmative, no problem," Hank replied. "I have the route in my HUD."

Cara bumped her, and when Diana turned to look at her, raised her hands. The message was clear. *See, I told you the mobile armory would be awesome.*

She rolled her eyes at her second in command and secured the Velcro straps that held her vest tight, then re-secured them when it failed to move comfortably with her when she twisted.

"Okay, people. Here's the deal. We're heading in to take on the enemy in their home base. Fortunately, they're not likely to be expecting us, and they didn't exactly choose the location for defensibility." She turned to face her team and rested one hand on top of the lockers and the other on the handle of the storage bin above the bench. "We'll helicopter in, blow holes in the roof, and rappel down. Watch the crossfires and keep track of where your teammates are on your map." There were nods accompanied by a few looks of concern, but mostly expressions of eager anticipation.

Diana grinned. "The good part is that this is exactly the kind of thing we're best at. They won't be able to cast spells from a distance because there will be no distance. Load up exclusively anti-magic for this one, and we should be able to eliminate half the threat reasonably quickly. Okay, team assignments—Khan and Hercules, Stark and Face, and Croft, Rambo, and I. The three of us will charge through the chaos and work toward wherever the lead witch is and eliminate her, and we'll deal with whoever is in the way. That leaves everyone else for you."

Tony laughed. "Call us the garbage men because we're taking out the trash."

Groans answered him, along with Kayleigh's muttered, "You are such an idiot, Stark," which generated more good-natured mirth.

"Okay, one more bad part. There's no way to know how fast they'll prep, so it's possible that instead of raiding a group milling about getting stuff together for an operation, we'll wind up against an actual fighting force, equipped and ready to roll. Neither option changes what we have to do. Every last one of them needs to be accounted for so we can put this thing to bed. If there are any escapees, Glam has them with the drones, so don't risk yourself to catch any runners."

Cara raised her hand, and Diana shook her head with a groan. "What?"

"How about we simply funnel them all outside and let the drones do the work?" A smattering of insults and shouts answered the facetious question so that she didn't have to, and she turned back to her locker. "Hercules, ETA?"

"Five and a quarter to the landing pad."

"Okay, y'all. Five minutes to get ready before we kick it into high gear."

She felt her back to ensure that the Bowie knife was in its proper position and loaded her vest and belt with spare magazines for her pistol and rifle. A tap verified the healing and energy flasks were where they were supposed to be. She snapped her fingers. "Grenades. Rambo, make sure every team has at least one smoke grenade and at least one flash-bang. They should protect our entry."

"Yep." The troll jumped from where he stood on the bench and ran the few steps to the rack on the wall to gather several of each.

Her shock gloves went on next, and she attached the line from under her sleeve to the connector that would recharge the energy in them. She removed Fury from the locker, detached the strap, and slid the sword and sheath awkwardly over her shoulder. After a few attempts, she found the top loop that Kayleigh had added to her vest and managed to slide it down at the correct angle to catch the other. When it was done, the Katana's hilt protruded over her right shoulder, positioned for a quick grasp and forehand attack. *It's yet another thing I haven't had enough time to practice with. But, hey, there's no time like the middle of a battle with a room full of enemies and a psycho witch, right?*

Diana donned her glasses and information flowed across her vision. The truck lurched to a stop, and the back doors opened when triggered from inside the cab. She strode forward, selected a rifle, and looped its carry line over her head before she leapt out and moved aside to allow the rest of the team to emerge. Hank jogged from the front and closed the doors when they were all out, then opened one of the low storage containers that were built under the floor of the passenger compartment. He withdrew four magnets, handed one to each team, and carried the extra himself. It was exactly like the man to bring a backup in case one of his meticulously maintained primaries failed. The agents turned and raced toward the chopper, keeping their heads low to avoid the unnaturally quiet rotors.

The aircraft lifted off as soon as they were all on board. They stood, grasping handholds mounted in the ceiling, and a National Guard soldier helped them drape the ropes they'd use for the building entry over a shoulder and under an arm to ensure it wouldn't hinder their exit from the aircraft. She handed each of them the safety line they would have during their descent to the structure. The plan was for the pilot to pull up fast and close enough that they could jump down, but it never hurt to have a backup in case something went wrong.

If they have a wizard on the roof playing sentry, this could go downhill in a hurry. She banished the thought. *Kayleigh would have alerted us already or simply stunned him.* The tech hadn't put any of the drones' feeds into their glasses, but she was confident that the woman maintained constant surveillance.

The team was silent as they flew through the dark skies. The wind whipped in one open side of the helicopter and out the other. Anik handed out shaped charges to use on the roof, and Cara took the one for the three of them. Because they'd be using the same magnet, they'd need to go down in sequence rather than all at once, but she hadn't wanted to add any more moving pieces to the mix.

The pilot's voice crackled over the speakers mounted in the bulkheads. "One minute. Everything looks clear for a hover-and-go."

Diana searched for something inspirational to say but couldn't come up with anything perfect, so she went with honesty instead. "People, this fight has been long, hard, and annoying for all of us. But finally, we have our opportunity to eliminate them all and rid our city of their threat. Nylotte will prevent them from being able to portal away." She'd received a telepathic message that her teacher was in position several minutes before. "All that's required is that we go in there and do what we do best. Watch out for each other and don't overreach. By the time this operation is done, you owe me every member of this bloody group dealt with. Prisoners are fine but don't risk yourselves to get them. They started the killing, so they've earned whatever end fate determines they should have."

There was a respectful silence until Tony quipped, "Do

it for Cara's motorcycle. It was one day away from retirement."

Laughter ensued, and Diana shook her head in mock despair. The pilot announced, "Fifteen seconds," and she waved her team into position. She shouted, "We are the Blackops Agents of Magic. Let's get in there and kick some criminal ass."

CHAPTER THIRTY-ONE

The helicopter tilted and descended abruptly and the speed change made the view outside the open door smear strangely. Diana had an instant where she thought she saw her teacher hiding in the trees nearby but wasn't positive. A stomach-dropping lurch made her catch her breath when the aircraft pulled out of its dive to hover above the roof. The agents jumped the three feet to the surface. Rath added a mid-air somersault to his leap, and the chopper veered away. She pointed for Anik and Hank to take the area to their left, Tony and Sloan to run to the right, and she, Cara, and the troll positioned themselves above the center. *If we had more people, we could have simply dropped directly into the office, but as it is, that would raise the danger level for the others way too high. Maybe once these losers are done with, we can expand.*

Her hands worked as her mind wandered, securing lines to the magnet while Cara placed the explosive. When she was done, she ran through the roll call, and each of her agents reported ready. "Okay, explosives, then grenades, then get in there and don't stop until they're destroyed. On three." She counted down and they detonated the charges together. One member of each team threw canisters into the hole, and the sound of the explosions was swallowed in the yelling and screaming that suddenly erupted below. Tony had suggested simply grenading the hell out of them, but with magic in play, they could possibly face the projectiles boomeranging, so she'd nixed the idea. She grinned at her teammates. "See you inside."

Diana jumped into the hole and gripped the line one hand and both feet to control the speed of her descent. It took only seconds for the transit and she wasn't able to get a good sense of the battlefield in so short a time. She landed, stepped away from the position to clear the way for the next person, and raised her weapon in barely enough time to direct a burst at a witch who wandered in front of her, choking from the smoke and bleeding from an ear. The bullets spun her and she fell and blood pooled beneath her.

"Sonic out." She threw one grenade and then the other toward where she thought the magicals would have been clustered based on Sloan's descriptions of the facility. The haze interfered with her lines of sight and limited what could have been a mass melee into a much more focused affair. She was sure the others would feel the same.

Rath and Cara appeared at her side, and she pointed forward. Clipped communication in her ear confirmed that the other teams had cleared their initial landing zones and engaged the closest enemies. Her team strode ahead and turned a corner formed by a six-foot stack of crates to where three opponents had dug in behind hastily improvised barricades. Bullets forced the BAM team to find cover, Diana and Rath to one side of the lane and Cara to the other. She tossed her last flash-bang, only to see it rebound into view almost immediately. She used her telekinesis to hurl it upward, and it detonated high enough that it didn't bother them, although the sound of breaking glass accompanied the blast. *I hope that was the office. Take that, witch.* She grinned as her earpieces picked up a wizard yelling about not being able to create a portal. A shriek of pain punctuated his sentence. *Way to draw attention to yourself, idiot.*

She pointed at Rath and gestured upward, and the troll clambered agilely to the lip of the crates and hung by his fingertips, ready to move. She whispered, "Go, Croft," and Cara whipped into the lane, fired her rifle, and raced forward. Diana stepped in behind her and used force magic to jolt the weapon from one defender's hand, then attempted her telekinetic wand-grab. She was almost shocked when it worked but the wizard in question was literally shocked when Rath soared toward him and discharged his batons into the man's chest. The other rifleman fired at Cara, but she'd already dropped into a slide. The couple of rounds that might have threatened Diana were deflected by a force shield she summoned to her left hand.

The troll attacked the unarmed man and swung his batons at sensitive places with noisy cracking sounds. Cara darted up and planted the stock of her rifle in the man's face when his magazine ran dry. Diana looked for a new foe and located two wizards about a dozen feet away who moved in a crouch toward the exit, using the stacked crates of stolen goods to hide. *Not good enough, guys.* She used a force blast to elevate herself, which elicited a shout of alarm from somewhere behind her before she arced to land a little beyond their next turn. When they appeared, she smiled.

"Hey, fellas." She rushed in before they could react, caught the one on the right in the jaw with a hook punch delivered with the loud snap of the shock gloves and lashed a kick at the other man's groin. He summoned a shadow shield to block it and snapped the magic disc at her face.

She backtracked a few steps to avoid it and cursed at the appearance of her least favorite form of magic so early in the battle. It got worse when tentacles erupted from his other arm but before she could panic, Fury whispered in her mind that he was well able to handle shadow. She drew the sword and swung it smoothly to chop through the translucent, grasping limbs and spun into a strike at her adversary's head. He lifted the shield and it had enough power to stop the blade. The defense also left his body open, however, so she tried the kick again and this time, it connected. He staggered back in pain and his defenses failed. She hammered him in the face with the hilt of the weapon and punched him with her shock glove. He collapsed with a groan.

Diana slid Fury into its scabbard and looked around. Even in the battle display, which had dots for friend and foe, it was difficult to sense the flow of the fight. They were still outnumbered but hopefully, the chaos would hold for long enough that her team could thin out the opposition before they could coordinate a defense. Rath dashed past her and she heard a yell of pain from the direction in which he had headed. *The cute tiny troll I found has become an absolute monster of a fighter. Who would have imagined that?* She scanned the battlefield for Sarah but didn't see either her or magic that could be connected to her. A little disappointed, she selected an enemy dot on the map nearby and stalked toward it, ready to do her part to even the numbers a little more.

Hank had lost track of Anik early in the battle, but the demolitions expert had assured him he was fine over their shared channel. The other man's fighting preferences were substantially less direct than his own, and he imagined that he'd found cover and simply waited for an opportunity to unleash trouble. *Me, on the other hand? Covert is totally not my style.* They'd landed in a gaggle of witches and wizards and he had eliminated the first few with bullets and the others with fists and feet, his magical reservoir surging with each contact. He'd taken a couple of blasts of magic but his vest had absorbed them, much to the shocked dismay of the casters. Now, he marched purposefully through the lanes created by the crates in search of criminals in need of his particular brand of justice.

He found a trio of witches and they raised their wands together as soon as they saw him. To their surprise, he barreled forward into their blasts. His vest consuming all of them and he landed a punch in the face of the woman closest to him and head-butted the person beside her. The third released a wash of fire and it was absorbed with the sound of cracking deflectors. He drew on the power he'd built up, increased his speed so her next attack missed, and pounded into her at a run. She catapulted into a set of crates, her momentum enough to break most of her bones and topple the tower. He turned his attention to the one he'd disoriented with his forehead strike and tapped her with a gentle punch that shocked her into unconsciousness. The dots on his display were diminishing, which was good. All those for allies were in motion, which was even better.

Bullets thudded into him from both sides, and he jerked his head up and scowled at two gunmen who had laid in wait and apparently, used the magicals as bait. *Heh. I wonder if they knew they were the cheese in the trap?* One of the rounds burned into his right shoulder and another caught him in the back of the left leg, and he lurched to the side and out of their firing line. The discomfort from the projectiles his vest had stopped was barely noticeable. While he took a moment to expend a trace of his magic to stem the blood flow and dull the pain, he didn't have time to dig the bullets out. He drew his Glock and his Ruger and stepped out again with the weapons extended at arms' length at either side, hoping they'd been too stupid to move. His wish was answered, and he emptied both weapons at them before they could react to his sudden reappearance. He shook his head as he changed the magazine in his pistol and stowed the revolver. *Thank all that is holy that we don't have mandatory military service, or these people might actually be dangerous.*

A fleeing human ran up beside him, saw who he was, and shrieked. Hank pistoned a side punch into his face and added a little magic into it, and the man's scream was cut off abruptly and he dropped like a stone. *Morons.* The agent strode forward in search of the next person who wanted to make the mistake of attacking him.

Cara dragged in a breath and realized that she was alone and suddenly surrounded. Her rifle was empty, and the five people who circled her all held wands. The daggers crowed with joy in her mind and urged her to set them loose. *Who am I to argue?* She grinned, drew them from the sheaths on her thighs, and surged into motion. The magicals cast spells that her vest sucked up and the deflectors cracked with a single loud pop when they were all consumed by the initial barrage. By then, she had broken out of the center and was already attacking the first of the enemy. Demon, in her left hand as always, stabbed the arm the woman raised in defense. Angel, in her right, snuck through to stab the inside elbow of her wand arm. The witch screamed as the agent spun away to the next person in line. She slipped past him, continued to spin until she was on the far side of the man, and brought her right arm around the back of his neck. Before he could react, she hurled him forward and into the path of the cone of fire the quickest witch had launched at her a second before.

He shouted in pain and stumbled blindly as the flames washed over him. She faced the third one—a witch again— as she grinned and fired a bolt of lightning. Cara laughed as her vest grounded it, then hissed in anger when shadow tentacles erupted from the woman's other arm. *Why always artifacts, and why always tentacles?* While she didn't have

Diana's almost obsessive dislike of the tactic, she wasn't a fan, either. Fortunately, her daggers were well able to slice through them, and she closed the distance and punched the woman in the mouth to deliver her brand of electrical charge with a snap of the shock gloves.

Angel screamed a warning in her mind, and Cara fell instinctively, ducked under the burning cone that sought her, and rolled away behind an obstacle as the witch tracked it along her path. *Okay, two left, plus the wounded one.* She moved rapidly to the far side of the tower, careful to avoid notice. The dots on her map didn't move, aside from the staggering wizard, which suggested that they continued to look for her. She crept behind the flame-throwing woman and, with a twinge at the unfairness of it, hurled Demon. He struck in the middle of her back and she screamed and went down. Cara clenched her fist, and the dagger dragged out of her target's body and returned to her hand, increasing the volume and frequency of her hoarse shouts.

She saw the final member of the group and launched fire darts at him. He recoiled and dropped his wand, and she lunged forward to punch both him and the burned man into unconsciousness. She turned, ran into the smoke, and sheathed the daggers before she shoved a new magazine into her rifle as she headed toward several dots that had gathered together and now moved in the direction of the exit.

Sarah had received a mental message from Iressa—the first

that hadn't required her to leave her physical form to pay homage to the woman—moments before the chaos below had begun. She'd tried to portal out immediately but had found her magic blocked. Irritated, she'd cast a few fire-balls into the fray from the staircase to ensure that it was only that particular spell that was affected before she retreated into her office to watch the battle. Part of her brain screamed in frustration, but another part took the invasion in stride. She laughed at herself at the passing wish that Marcus, the walking arsenal, was still around to help her. The witch honestly wasn't afraid. Fear had been left behind during her escape from the World in Between. But she had a dark feeling about this new development as if the fate she'd believed in for so long was revealed to be only a dream and this was what things were like when awake.

Her superior had checked in after the first few minutes, and she'd let the woman know about the blocked portal. Sarah had spent the time since then keeping an eye on the battle and preparing for it to reach her. She kept her wand in her hand, made sure her backup was in easy reach at the small of her back, and put on the armor her patron had provided her. It was leather and chainmail, with a few light impact plates here and there. It also had a number of magic deflectors attached, borrowing an idea from the enemy.

Their leader, Sheen, emerged from the smoke and violence below to stand at the bottom of the stairs and look up. With a muttered oath, Sarah yanked her head away from the window and moved to stand behind the door and peer through the peephole. The woman seemed to consider the risks involved with ascending the staircase as she remained where she was and shook her head. Her lips moved but it was impossible to make out what she was saying. Suddenly, she elevated and her arc launched her directly toward the door the witch hid behind.

She backpedaled into the room as the woman pounded into the door. It held, thanks to the wards and defenses she'd added to it. In truth, she probably would have let her foe climb the stairs without contest rather than open it. *Hopefully, she hurt herself.* It took only a half-minute before the door finally catapulted off its hinges to slam into the back wall of the office. The enemy stood silhouetted in the doorway, and she summoned a line of fire and trained it on her. Sheen blocked it with a fire shield, and Sarah cursed. Then, Iressa's voice whispered good news in her mind, and she grinned. She deactivated her attack and readied her defense, but the other woman chose to speak.

"How about you come quietly?" *She sounds tired.*

Rather than respond, she cast a spell at the desk in front of her to transform it into a projectile that rocketed toward her enemy. Sheen responded with a force blast to redirect it and another aimed at her that was absorbed by her deflectors. In the moment of distraction it brought, she conjured a portal at her feet and fell through to safety.

CHAPTER THIRTY-TWO

"What the actual fuck!" Diana's shout was involuntary and heartfelt. She managed to control her anger and yelled, "Rambo, get outside and make sure our secret weapon is okay. The damn witch portaled out of here. Glam, do we know where she went?" *One break. One break is all I need. Come on, fate.*

The tech answered in seconds. "She's in her apartment —rushing around by the looks of it."

The agent reviewed the portal locations she knew and shook her head in frustration. Nothing was close. "How long by chopper to get there?"

"Minutes."

"Okay, I'm headed to the roof. Bring it in and have them lower a line."

She looked up through a hole that existed in the drywall that was once the ceiling of the room and saw the metal roof of the structure far above. "'Copter ETA?"

"Thirty seconds."

So they're not overhead. Good. She extended her hands

241

and fired flame at the metal to burn through it in an instant. Her force magic enabled her to half-leap and half-fly up and out of the hole to land cleanly on the surface before she ran to its highest point. The running lights of the aircraft were visible as it raced toward her. "Croft, I'm going after Sarah. Finish this here."

"Affirmative."

Rath's voice came over the line. "Secret weapon had to defend self. Is fine now."

Okay, then, it's only me and you, bitch. The rope spilled out of the chopper as it passed low over the roof, and Diana grabbed it and held on. It hauled her up and away and swung her in a wide pendulum motion as it reoriented toward the downtown building that housed her enemy's apartment. The flight was equal parts frightening and exhilarating, but both feelings were at a remove, her entire being focused on bringing an end to Sarah before she could escape again.

Kayleigh sounded angry. "She's clearly packing stuff, boss. She plans to run."

"She won't have the opportunity. Tell Nylotte she needs to get close enough to block that."

Rath replied, "She's on her way. Asks if you need help."

She bared her teeth in a grin. "Hell no. There's no chance she'll get away from me again."

The pilot's voice was crackly as it joined the comms channel. "Roof landing?"

Diana thought it through. It was certainly the most reasonable and rational means of entry. Land, tie off, and rappel down to come in through a window. *Okay, screw reasonable. We'll do it the fun way.* "No, here's what I want you to do."

The building came up fast. Kayleigh had already summoned police and fire in case there was fallout from the fight and had ordered the doorman to quietly evacuate the floors under Sarah's. The National Guard soldier on the aircraft had adjusted the rope length, and Diana managed to get her boot wedged in the loop at the bottom in the few minutes of flight that had brought them to this moment. The tech warned her that the woman seemed almost done packing, but the agent had received word from Nylotte that she was in place moments before. The witch couldn't go anywhere unless it was on foot. *I would love to fight her in the elevator. That would be amazing. How about it, fate, two-for-two?*

"Final approach," announced the pilot, and the helicopter surged with a burst of speed, tilted, and suddenly stopped. The maneuver swung her smoothly toward the windows of Sarah's living room. The idea had come from watching the video of the woman almost throwing a chair through them, and once it had taken hold, Diana knew it was the only way to do it. She extended a hand and directed blasts of force ahead of her to shatter the window before she reached it. In the next second, she leapt from the rope to slide cleanly into the chamber and hurdled over the coffee table that was pushed away from where it belonged in the middle of the couches.

"Sarah, we didn't get to finish our conversation," she yelled. "Maybe you'd like to now."

There was no reply, and Kayleigh chuckled. "Yeah, she tried to portal but it didn't work. She looks seriously angry."

"Oh, is your escape plan not working?" the agent continued. "How sad. Will you come out, or do I have to come in there to get you?"

The witch emerged from the hallway with a wand in each hand and as intense an expression as Diana had ever seen stretched over her face. Truly, at this moment, she looked every bit as insane as they'd joked she was. Her voice was harsh and almost hoarse as she snarled, "You are nothing. I will enjoy killing you and I will revel in killing everyone you've ever known, starting with your blonde girlfriend the idiot Dreven failed to eliminate."

Diana shook her head. "We're past threats, aren't we?"

"That's not a threat. It's a promise. A vow. A damned fact."

A memory of her battle with Fury came to mind. She said, "I'd offer you one more chance to end this peacefully, but I know you wouldn't take it."

"Die, bitch." Sarah flicked both wands at her, and Diana summoned shields of fire to absorb the shadow bolts that hurtled toward her. Her foe crossed the room toward the kitchen, perhaps trying to angle toward the door, but she remained in step with her and simply focused on maintaining her defenses until the woman made a mistake. When the tentacles erupted from her arm, the agent was ready and summoned a force blade to slash them away and turned it into an attack, hurling the object at the witch.

The second set of tentacles that emerged from her adversary's other arm were a complete surprise and had already wound around her legs before she fully processed their appearance.

She snatched Fury's hilt, drew the blade smoothly, and sliced the weapon through them, but more appeared and she was hard-pressed to keep up with them. Shadow bolts filled the spaces between, and Diana fell into a rotation of blocks and swipes. She managed to avoid damage but found no openings to counter. The sword coached her and helped her to make the right movements, and she felt confident she could maintain the stalemate. The other woman's face was locked in a superior, crazed grin. Diana had an instant in which she realized she was being played before the couch careened into her from the side— summoned while she was distracted by the shadow attacks —and she reeled into the kitchen area from the impact and fell. Her sword skittered away.

She scrambled to her feet in time to thrust more incoming objects aside with her own force blasts. The sense of having taken all she was willing to take from the witch swamped her, suffused her, and filled each and every cell to bursting. Icicles exploded from her extended fist, but the woman's deflectors absorbed them before they cracked with a familiar snap as they were consumed. She sent a wave of force at her adversary, which pushed the tentacles away and hurled her against the undamaged window, which held and bounced her back into the room. The witch climbed to her feet and blood seeped from a small cut on the side of her head. Sarah snarled. "Lucky shot. It'll be your last."

Rather than bother to reply, she turned the woman's tactic against her, caught objects with her telekinesis, and flung them at her. Her shadow tentacles deflected most of them and the rest fell to her wands, but Diana was now the one in control. The hail of cutlery she launched at the woman was particularly pleasing, and a paring knife snuck through to stab her in the shoulder. The witch yanked it out with a growl and threw it back at her, but the agent had found her bearings. She threw several large objects and forced the other woman to move sideways. *Only a little further.*

Sarah rallied and managed another eruption of tentacles, but her opponent was ready. She held her hand out and Fury responded to spiral across the room and into her grasp. The serpentine attackers were severed quickly. The next wave met the same fate, as did the shadow bolts before a smug look sidled onto the witch's face again, which doubtless heralded some clever idea that had occurred to her. However, it also indicated a moment of distraction. Diana extended her telekinesis and dragged the woman's leading foot forward to upset her balance. She saw the look of fear as the force punch that followed thumped into her chest and in the next second, Sarah soared backward out the window. Tentacles reached frantically to grab at anything to stop her fall, but the agent strode to the opening and shredded them. The enemy witch plummeted with a long, terrified shriek that only ceased when she impacted with the blockaded street below. *Finally.*

Diana turned and sheathed Fury. Kayleigh said, "Damn. Nice fight, boss. I thought she had you."

She laughed. "For a minute there, I did too. But I think she was crazy enough that it compromised her ability to fight. Which was probably good for all of us."

"True that."

"How do things stand at the warehouse?"

There was a definite tone of satisfaction in the tech's voice. "All enemies have been captured or killed, as near as we can tell. A few made it out to be stunned. The team is on the way back to base."

The agent turned, looked out the window at the headquarters building a couple of blocks away, and pictured her team returning in victory. Finally, the Remembrance was destroyed. "I'll be right there." She tried to open a portal and discovered she couldn't. With a sigh, she headed to the door to find Nylotte and tell her that she could stop blocking. "Okay, correction, I'll be there soon."

CHAPTER THIRTY-THREE

A sense of palpable relief had hung over the ARES HQ in the days since the battle at the warehouse and the subsequent fight in the head witch's ritzy condo. They'd all taken varying amounts of time off or engaged in essential tasks that had fallen by the wayside as they battled the Remembrance. Diana and Rath had spent a couple of days in DC with Bryant and Lisa, then she'd ensconced herself in a room with Kayleigh and Cara for a day to work on an after-action summary of the most recent month fighting the Remembrance. They'd have to do a more extensive one to close the chapter on the organization, but everyone agreed that the task could wait a while.

She'd visited Nylotte in the kemana, and her teacher had apologized—actually apologized—for not seeing the potential hazards of her involvement. The Dark Elf had moved between regret and anger when she described the appearance of the dark witch Iressa and the need to defend herself from the woman's sudden attack. In retrospect, they probably should have considered the possibility, but they'd been so focused on what was in front of them that it had never occurred to anyone. Diana doubted the witch would leave the Drow's thoughts anytime soon, however.

An hour each day was devoted to working with Fury on imaginary battlefields of his creation, absorbing what he had to teach her about swordplay tactics and strategies. Her body moved, teaching the muscles, but most of it occurred in her mind. Nonetheless, when she was finished, she was always sweating and trembling as if every stroke of the virtual battles had been real. She had also joined Cara for several training sessions with Nylotte now that time permitted, and they were both learning to find the line between effectiveness and energy expenditure that worked for them. Both her teacher and her sword promised that, over time, she would be able to store power in the artifact for later use.

Today was the first time they would all be in one place since the event, and Diana had reserved the back room at Stan's again. Somehow, it seemed fitting, despite Cara's contention that celebrations and champagne were synonymous. She yelled for Rath and Kayleigh as she located her car keys. The troll raced in with Max on his heels, laughing as the dog snapped at him. One of the best things about the house was the large backyard where the two of them could tussle when they felt the need. The tech emerged from the basement, looking as happy and relaxed as she'd been in ages.

"Did you win?"

She snorted. "Of course I did. But the competition during the daylight hours is weak."

Diana nodded, having no idea what she was talking

about but happy that she seemed pleased. "Cool. Or whatever the kids say these days. Let's get a move on."

They climbed into her Mustang Fastback, the troll took his place on the booster in the admittedly tiny back seat, and she started the engine. She drove as cautiously as required but also put a little extra speed into turns and straight runs for the sheer joy of it. When they finally reached the restaurant, Kayleigh was hoarse from telling her to slow down, their diminutive companion was laughing giddily, and she had burned away what was left of her stress. They entered through the rear door and found that Stan had provided a curtain rather than only the rope to keep their celebration private.

A table with heating trays stood loaded with barbecue and sides, and they filled their plates. Everyone did the same as they arrived, and the group ate with deep satisfaction, seated around a large rectangular table, and shared laughs and tales of their past adventures. Finally, Tony and Deacon stood on their seats and called for everyone's attention. The tech said, "We have gathered here to put the recent past behind us. And there's only one true way to do that. Awards!"

The investigator jumped down and opened a box to reveal a number of cheesy trophies with stars on them. The assembled group laughed, and he turned to them with a grin. "First up, for constant whining on someone else's behalf...Kayleigh!" Amidst the cheers, she walked up to collect her trophy with a look in her eyes that promised agony for Deacon. He seemed unimpressed and announced the next award.

"For the most elegant design in battle vehicles since the

Transformers...Hank!" Applause thundered from every-one, clearly sincere, and he stretched to take the award from where he sat, looking both pleased and uncomfortable in equal measures.

Tony bellowed, "Best at opening doorways in unconventional ways...Anik!" More laughter followed as the demolitions expert made his way to the front.

The tech grinned. "Best gunslinger impersonation, including the ridiculous mustache...Tony!" He laughed off the jeers as he accepted the award from his fellow presenter.

"Biggest techno-weenie on Earth...Deacon!"

Kayleigh shouted, "Well-deserved!" and the others laughed again.

Diana leaned over to Cara. "I'm a little worried that they're leaving us for last."

The other woman nodded. "We should make a run for it."

Tony calmed everyone and fixed them with a somber look. "But seriously, now, a few more. First, for conduct far beyond the line of duty and putting himself in harm's way for the benefit of the team...Sloan." Their respect for the man was obvious in their applause, and he seemed to take it to heart.

Deacon added, "For caring far beyond the line of duty and truly watching over the place where we live...Rath." The troll ran forward and flipped dramatically, making the onlookers laugh, but the emotional weight in the room doubled with the reminder of his efforts to help the local Griffins. The man continued, "And for accepting her position in the crosshairs when our enemies tried to kill her not once, but twice, while we waited for the right moment...Cara." Diana felt tears of pride welling in the corners of her eyes as her second in command went to accept her trophy. *Dammit. I could not be prouder of these people.*

Tony gave her a solemn look from the other end of the table. "And for being a thrill-seeking maniac who clearly wants to be a superhero...our fearless leader, Diana!" The crowd whooped and hooted, then raised their bottles in a toast to her. She raised her own. "To you all. The best team anyone has ever had the privilege to lead." She paused to let that sink in, then added, "Except for Tony, whose ass I will now kick." He laughed and jogged toward the exit, where she caught him and gave him a hug. "Great work, Stark. That was exactly what we needed."

He mimed spinning pistols and holstering them, and they returned to the party.

On another planet, Lechnas and Iressa sat together near the fire once again. The witch had arrived with a sense of trepidation covering her like an aura but had marshaled her reserves when she saw him seated calmly and waiting and had slid into the chair beside him with something approaching her usual confidence. The offer of whiskey had been quickly accepted and seemed to bolster her spirits.

He spoke slowly and kept his emotions hidden. In truth, he had anticipated that their people on Earth would fail, although he had hoped they would at least cause a little

TR CAMERON

more trouble before their elimination. "So. The witch failed us."

She looked up with a startled expression that she quickly covered up. *Yes, us.* There was relief in her voice. "She did. I intervened, of course, but could only do so much. It gave her a fighting chance but in the end, the enemy leaders foiled us again."

"And the rumored demise of the first target was apparently in error." That mistake was his. When Pesharn did not return, he should have known the attempt failed—or, at least, assumed it had. Instead, he had trusted in his sources in the government agencies, who turned out to have been manipulated with false information. *Even the most competent can misstep from time to time.*

Iressa nodded. "Yes. There was no inkling of the truth of that situation."

Lechnas leaned back and took a deep and appreciative sip of his drink before responding. "But, on the positive side, they believe they are now safe and that the threat has passed. We will let them enjoy that illusion for a time. Our actions will be subtle at first, using only those we can absolutely trust. But within the month, Stonesreach will fall, the city above will burn, and those leaders and all their people will beg for death at our hands."

The story doesn't end here. The team continues to go after the bad guys in <u>Agents of Vengeance</u>. You won't want to miss the exciting conclusion to the series!

CONNECT WITH TR CAMERON

Stay up to date on new releases and fan pricing by signing up for my newsletter. CLICK HERE TO JOIN.

Or visit: www.trcameron.com/Oriceran to sign up.

If you enjoyed this book, please consider leaving a review. Thanks!

AUTHOR NOTES - TR CAMERON

WRITTEN AUGUST 18, 2019

Every book makes the ride that much wilder. Thank you for coming along with us!

Thank you for reading the *seventh* book in the Federal Agents of Magic series, and for continuing on to the author notes! I am grateful every single day that you make it possible for me to share this story with you.

I spent this past weekend at a commitment ceremony / big party to celebrate my best friend's wedding last year. It was awesome, but also offered a lot of time for reflection.

Since finding my home with Martha, Michael, and LMBPN, what was a sometimes-scary solo pursuit has become a joyous adventure. The way the pieces came together was so unlikely that it feels like it was meant to be.

A few years back, I applied for a new job. I was excited for it, I saw it as a step forward and something I'd be good at and something that would increase the long-term security for my family. The downside was that it was going to require me to give up a lot of the freedoms I've worked pretty darn hard to attain for the last decade and a half or so, and if we're thinking about it broadly, for the last thirty years. Even as I applied, I was still torn about whether to take or not if it was offered.

It might have been worth it. But, fortunately, I didn't get it. I didn't even get interviewed, which was a clear lack of perspective on their parts, but I digress.

At the time, I was a little upset. But then I decided if that wasn't my path, I needed to figure out what was.

I don't recall what keyed me in to the existence of self-publishing, or the desire to turn my love of story into a writing career. It might actually have been the Kurtherian Gambit, but it's in a foggy rear view and I can't make it out. But the moment I discovered it, it felt like fate's hand at work.

So, I read a few things, listened to a podcast, sat my rear end down in the chair at 4am and started writing. After a week, I realized that I didn't know what the hell I was doing. Tell a good story, sure. But all the behind-the-scenes stuff that's important to make that story work? I had some learning to do.

I learned. I wrote. I threw stuff I loved away and tried again. And I think (hope?) I'm still improving with each new chapter I write.

What's the takeaway? That old saw that when one door closes another opens – more proof that it's more true than it is false.

Something new and cool is on the horizon, and I look forward to sharing it with you when it's ready for release!

If you want to chat media, the books, or whatever else, I check in pretty often on Facebook. Just search TR

Cameron Author to find me. Or, less reliably, thom@trcameron.com.

Now, back to plotting book 8, where Lechnas and Iressa… well, you'll have to wait and see.

Until next time, Joys upon joys to you and yours – so may it be.

AUTHOR NOTES - MARTHA CARR

AUGUST 21, 2019

The temperature is down to the mid 90's in Austin, Texas –
The Fall season must be approaching. A little Texas humor,
but also true. School is back in session here and I'm only
two weeks away from turning 60. I swear, I feel like I'm
about 30 years old. My author buddy, Craig Martelle paid
me a high compliment by saying, "I don't know what 60
should look like, but you don't look it – and you don't act
it either."

I'll be off to Niagara Falls for a long weekend on the
actual day because – why not? I've never seen them and
seems just weird enough for a Nerdette like me. Check that
one off the list of natural wonders to see!

I'm looking forward to my 60's, mostly because my 50's
have been the best decade of my life despite loss and struggles and large challenges that were mixed in with great and
wonderous changes. It was mostly because I learned how
to be happy despite circumstances and operate within a
community instead of muscling through every adventure
on my own.

I used to think happiness was dependent on circum-stances – I mean that makes sense, right? If times are tough, happiness seems rash or ignorant or maybe even a form of denial. But it's still possible.

For me, it takes reaching out to some trusted friends who are grounded in the same philosophy and listening more than I speak. I'm reminded of what's going right in my life and encouraged to take note of where I'm sitting, what I can see around me, what is the scent in the air, how does my body feel right this minute? That's called mindful-ness and for me, it's been a game changer. I've even learned how to apply it to what I'm eating (and fortunately, not eating so much).

That part about community – I grew up in a chaotic household where it was more – every man, woman and child for themselves. Asking questions was an opportunity for ridicule and abuse from others. I learned how to observe and be silent. But I kept a child's perspective all the way up to my 50's – that all I observed was all there was. Even though intellectually I knew there are a million different views to any topic, I operated as if mine was the only one – without realizing I was doing it.

It was at the beginning of my 50's that I started to ask more questions like, how do you do this, or what do you mean and found out – I don't know a lot of things – and it was welcome news. I became more curious – again – like I was five years old once more – and my internal optimism grew and surpassed my need to look for approaching trouble.

It also meant I was showing people more of who I really am, which led like a series of falling dominoes to finding my tribe of people who like me for who I am – and weeded out those who really didn't and needed to move on to another circle of friends. Everything became easier, even during the tough times because judgment was decreasing in degrees all the time. It still is and is a welcome relief.

That's why I'm looking forward to my 60's so much. I spent so many years holding back, being quiet and not finding out about all the things that interested me because I was so busy trying not to be noticed – to stay safe. But these days I'm flinging myself out there, even when I'm afraid or awkward or anxious and learning all kinds of cool things – in community – with a lot of great people (a lot of them are you guys). Imagine what the future holds... More adventures to follow.

AUTHOR NOTES - MICHAEL ANDERLE

AUGUST 28, 2019

THANK YOU for not only reading this story but these *Author Notes* as well.

(I think I've been good with always opening with "thank you." If not, I need to edit the other *Author Notes*!)

RANDOM (*sometimes*) THOUGHTS?

You can buy too much junk food.

I'm in Shanghai, China after a trip on a train that took about 15 hours. In preparation for this trip, my wife and I went to a grocery store run by a French company in Beijing China. It was similar to (in the US) a small Wal*Mart.

The store was laid out in a very long rectangle, taking up a floor beneath a strip center. We walked in one narrow side of the rectangle and had the WHOLE strip center to walk to get to the fruits / vegetables / meat.

Needless to say, I didn't make it past the junk food (chips) aisle before I was trying to figure out which chips I needed to take with me on the train.

I mean, salty is one of the main food groups, isn't it?

So, the next main food group is sweet and that meant… more junk food!

Our little basket started filling up, fast.

So, eventually we made our way to the middle of the food area in this store, and there were pink banners that I read 'Imported' on.

AH! Food from manufacturers I recognized. Chips Ahoy! (in the basket) – Lay's Potato Chips (in the basket). I had to make two trips to take back foods I thought I recognized, but wasn't sure, in order not to be stupid about buying food I did.

I grabbed Skittles, Snickers… the sugary craze went on and on…

Then, being mature adults, we started to look for something 'not' junk. Well, actually we didn't start looking until we found the peanut butter. Then, it was a freaking FULL store search effort to find grape jelly and plastic forks and knives to make our sandwiches with the bread we found.

We found close-enough jam but never found any plastic ware. All of the forks / knives / spoons were metal. Not exactly something I wanted to buy and have security take from me so we didn't buy any.

This trip was easily an hour or more trying to find the food 'just right' for the 15+ hours on the train.

A train that left at 8:00 PM at night.

In the end, we lugged two very large plastic bags of food from the store to the hotel, then to the train station, then through two security gates with scanners. We finally reached train itself where the food took up a lot of space in our tiny little compartment.

We ended up eating 1/2 a small plastic tub of popcorn and some skittles and sleeping most of the trip.

Oh, we also opened and drank two waters.

AROUND THE WORLD IN 80 DAYS

One of the interesting (at least to me) aspects of my life is the ability to work from anywhere and at any time. In the future, I hope to re-read my own *Author Notes* and remember my life as a diary entry.

Shanghai China, in the Executive Lounge Shanghai Marriot City Center.

I woke up at 2:30 PM.

Well, that's not true. I went to bed (local CST time) at 2:00 AM, alarm goes of at 8:15 AM to get on an 8:30 AM call for folks up and meeting at 8:30 PM back on the Eastern seaboard of the United States.

I'm awake until 10:30 AM getting some projects done and then go to bed thinking 'I'll try to take a small nap.'

I wake up almost five hours later, really not wanting to move at all.

BUT, these author notes need to be written so that Zen Master Walking(™) Steve can do a pre-order and hopefully correct a few Amazon issues of late.

I'm a bit mentally foggy, still. I'm going to allow Steve (ZMW™) to add a few comments about why he had me get out of bed in the middle of the afternoon to do this ;-)

<ZMW™ here. As you know, we (LMBPN) make a big effort to keep readers informed about book releases and sales. Normally, Amazon smiles on those efforts. We're

able to click the publish button and a few hours later the book is available to readers. Or, for Saturday Fan's Pricing, we change the prices mid-day on Friday, and Amazon has them on sale by Saturday.

Normally.

For the past two weeks, things have not been normal. Last week each of our books took between eight and ten hours to publish. Yesterday's book, ONE WITCH TOO FEW, took nearly 18 hours. And each of the past two weeks Fan Pricing days had at least one book that didn't price change for at least 24 hours.

So... Since next Thursday's book, ARCANE OPS, has been through the editing process, we decided to set it up as a pre-order to be sure it's released on schedule.

Easy peasy, right?

Well yes, except we needed Michael's author notes. And he and Judith have been on the road traveling for the past month, and it was one more thing I needed to ask for. (And this was before I learned about their heroic effort to buy and transport enough American junk food to feed the Chinese National Basketball Team over a 15 hour train ride.)

So, I took a chance and interrupted Michael's slumber *in the middle of the afternoon.*

He has forgiven me. I think ;)

Now, let's get back to our regularly scheduled author notes...>

FAN PRICING

$0.99 Saturdays (new LMBPN stuff) and $0.99 Wednesday (both LMBPN books and friends of LMBPN books.) Get great stuff from us and others at tantalizing prices.

Go ahead, I bet you can't read just one.

Sign up here: http://lmbpn.com/email/.

HOW TO MARKET FOR BOOKS YOU LOVE

Review them so others have your thoughts, tell friends and the dogs of your enemies (because who wants to talk with enemies?)... *Enough said ;-)*

Ad Aeternitatem,

Michael Anderle

OTHER SERIES IN THE ORICERAN
UNIVERSE:

SCHOOL OF NECESSARY MAGIC
SCHOOL OF NECESSARY MAGIC: RAINE CAMPBELL
ALISON BROWNSTONE
THE DANIEL CODEX SERIES
THE LEIRA CHRONICLES
I FEAR NO EVIL
FEDERAL AGENTS OF MAGIC
THE UNBELIEVABLE MR. BROWNSTONE
REWRITING JUSTICE
THE KACY CHRONICLES
MIDWEST MAGIC CHRONICLES
SOUL STONE MAGE
THE FAIRHAVEN CHRONICLES

OTHER BOOKS BY JUDITH BERENS

OTHER BOOKS BY MARTHA CARR

JOIN THE ORICERAN UNIVERSE FAN GROUP ON FACEBOOK!

Made in the USA
Las Vegas, NV
16 February 2023

67614699R00163